OMG

QUEER

Short Stories by Queer Youth

Visit us at www.boldstrokesbooks.com

OMG
QUEER
Short Stories by Queer Youth

edited by

RADCLY*f*FE and
KATHERINE E. LYNCH, PhD

A Division of Bold Strokes Books

2012

OMGQUEER: SHORT STORIES BY QUEER YOUTH
© 2012 BY BOLD STROKES BOOKS. ALL RIGHTS RESERVED.

ISBN 13: 978-1-60282-682-3

THIS TRADE PAPERBACK ORIGINAL IS PUBLISHED BY
BOLD STROKES BOOKS, INC.
P.O. BOX 249
VALLEY FALLS, NY 12185

FIRST EDITION: AUGUST 2012

CREDITS
EDITORS: RADCLYFFE, KATHERINE E. LYNCH, STACIA SEAMAN
PRODUCTION DESIGN: STACIA SEAMAN
COVER DESIGN BY SHERI (GRAPHICARTIST2020@HOTMAIL.COM)

Acknowledgments

This book would not have been possible without all of the hardworking and selfless people at Bold Strokes Books— Connie, Lori, Lee, Jennifer, Paula, Sheri, Cindy, Stacia, and others—who help to put out and market quality product year after year. Sandy deserves special thanks for keeping us well-organized. Finally, we would like to applaud the anthology contributors for their fine contributions to this collection.

To every individual who has made it their life's work to improve the quality of life for LGBTQI youth.

CONTENTS

INTRODUCTION

Stories are humanity's oldest communication tools. They allow us to explore new worlds and plumb the depths of the human mind. They offer us the catharsis of laughter and tears. They inspire us when we need to be lifted up and succor us when we need comfort. Most of all, stories create connections between individuals. They encourage the sharing of experiences, values, fears, and triumphs. They permeate borders, sometimes against great opposition. They defy the human lifespan and live on through millennia. They have the power to incite revolutions and to encourage peacemaking.

The stories in this anthology glean their power in part from the positions of their authors within society. Young, queer writers in the twenty-first century find themselves in a confusing world—an ambivalent reality in which the President of the United States announces his endorsement of marriage equality less than twenty-four hours after a majority of citizens in North Carolina vote to ban same-sex marriage. Perhaps now more than ever, queer individuals around the globe are called to share their experiences—not only in order to stand in solidarity with one another, but to communicate their hopes, dreams, and goals with people of every identity.

British author Rudyard Kipling wrote: "If history were told in the form of stories, it would never be forgotten." As you peruse the tales that follow, we invite you not only to appreciate them as stories in their own right, but to read them as artifacts of this tumultuous time for queer citizens of our planet. To tell our stories is to share our truths; to speak out is to become visible—and those who are visible are both harder to ignore and harder to oppress. These young authors reveal their selves in bravery and honesty, in pain and celebration, and we salute them.

We are everywhere. These are some of our stories.

—Katherine E. Lynch, PhD and Radclyffe, 2012

JELSON
BRENNA HARVEY

Everyone at school loved Jelson. I mean, rightly so, I love Jelson too. Jelson is my best friend. But I was really surprised. I figured being a Swop, especially the first Swop to ever go to Manetow High, would mean instant outcast status. And I'm not talking about the sad, lonely, no-one-talks-to-me-because-I-read-Sylvia-Plath-and-wear-a-neck-brace kind of outcast. I'm talking about graphic, illustrated death threats in your locker and violent sexual harassment in the bathroom. I'm talking about the kind of outcast who doesn't live to see senior prom.

But, like I said, everyone at school loved Jelson. I guess part of it was because we weren't a super-homophobic school. Little white town, rural Iowa, not rich, you'd think we'd keelhaul queers under our homecoming floats. But it turns out we were pretty good. We had a couple of out teachers. There was Ms. Barbiaz, this really cool butch social studies teacher who plastered her room with giant posters of Ruth Bader Ginsberg. And we had Mr. Niddio, our totally flaming drama instructor. He made us do a lot of trust exercises and he would actually tear up if he heard someone use the word *fag*. Kids still used it, but they felt like total shit about it if Mr. Niddio heard them.

We also had a Gay-Straight Alliance that the administration supported. The only people who went regularly were Tony Peluzzi, our one actual real live dude-kissing gay boy, and some combination of the dozen girls who followed him around and claimed him as their best friend. I went to a couple meetings, but it was mostly girls vying to sit on Tony's lap and asking him to do their makeup.

I should have figured that if Tony never got punched for wearing eyeliner, Jelson would be okay. I just assumed being a Swop would be different—would freak everyone out way more. I mean, people justify hating on gays because gay people are supposedly all threatening to the established social order and families and precious little babies or whatever. Since, you know, if we all turn gay we'll forget who should be employed and who should breastfeed and all the babies will starve to death and litter our suburban sidewalks with tiny, tragic skeletons. So if gay people are threatening to society, then what about Swops? Medical anomalies who can change biological sex at will? That's like, gay squared. Dodecagay. Infinigay. So gay it gays all the way around the world to gay again. In the butt.

But people got over Jelson being a Swop pretty fast. I guess all Ms. Barbiaz's lectures about gay and transgender and intersex rights movements actually had an effect on the student body. Mr. Niddio's interpretive dances on the same topics were undoubtedly less helpful, but they certainly spiced up school talent shows. Honestly, kids were way weirder to Keith Lamar, our one black kid, about not being on the basketball team than they ever were to Jelson. Man, it would have been nice if we'd had some black teachers.

I'm probably making it sound like the honest efforts of

some tenacious, well-meaning educators made our school some kind of big gay tolerance rainbow disco utopia. But I'm leaving out one extremely important detail. Namely, the fact that Jelson is totally hot. Like, staggeringly, painfully hot. And not only that, but Jelson is equally hot as both a boy and a girl. And not hot like people you see on TV. Jelson is more like this subtle kind of sexy, sort of slender and dark and mysterious. It's a special look. I think it has a lot to do with playful smiles. And expressive eyebrows. And eyes that look smart. Anyway, Jelson's raging sexiness definitely helped a whole bunch when it came to sliding into the social order at Manetow.

And I'm allowed to talk about Jelson's hotness as a totally objective outside observer. Jelson's my best friend, and my own sexuality is way too messed up for me to actually be attracted to a real live hot girl or a real live hot boy. What I mean is, my appreciation of Jelson's beauty is purely aesthetic. I look at the line of his boy-jaw, or watch the purse of her girl-lips, and I see the beauty there. But it's kind of like admiring the curve of a tree branch or the top of a Roman column or something. Jelson says I'm an asexual in denial. I say Jelson should just split into two people and they can go fuck themselves.

Personally, I think it's funny the way boys and girls go apeshit over Jelson at different times. It's not like Jelson even changes much when going from girl to boy. There's no comic boob inflation sequence, no funny instant beard sprout. Jelson keeps the same slim-hipped, athletic body. Same light brown skin, same short dark hair. Sure, she gets these cute little perky breasts as a girl, and his upper arms beef up a little as a boy, but we're not talking Jekyll and Hyde here. To me, it seems mostly like a movement thing. She'll flutter her eyelashes a little more when she's a girl, or shift his weight down, thrust his pelvis out a little more as a boy. It's mostly about signals. Like, "Hey, you, you're allowed to be attracted to me now. Come and get it."

But what do I know? Like I said, sexual attraction is a complicated and mysterious animal to me. The differences between boys and girls, their distinct shapes and sounds, these don't excite me. Six-pack abs or hourglass figures, they seem so extreme, like you have to squish a human being up and press them in a mold to get them to look that way. What I'm trying to say is that I really don't get conventional standards of hotness for boys and girls. And I certainly don't understand why people react so differently to Jelson on days when she wears a bra and days when he has a stubbly little mustache.

The only thing I can truly understand getting hot and bothered over are Jelson's eyes. Big, sparkling, intelligent-looking eyes. They create this witty, knowing look. I will never understand people who can tolerate stupid-looking eyes.

"Oh my God, everyone in this magazine looks totally brain dead," I muttered, leafing through a copy of *Rage* during free period. It was early fall, but still warm, so Jelson and I were lounging on the picnic tables outside the cafeteria. It's a shit spot, just a plain cement terrace with a scenic view of the parking lot and some trees that look super-depressed about the state of American public education. But you get some sun and you can play music if you're not a dick about it.

"I hope you didn't pay money for that, Allie," said Jelson. He'd kicked off his sandals and was sitting barefoot and cross-legged on the opposite bench, frowning at me. He was doing this seriously judgmental thing with his eyebrows that's usually reserved for daytime talk shows and student government campaign speeches. He was a boy today but reading a copy of *Mrs. Dalloway* because he's like that.

"No, I took it from the library," I said.

"Took like borrowed or took like stole?"

"Well, they won't let you take magazines out of the room. Anyway, check this out." I held up the page I was looking at. It was a photo of some vacant blond girl in a velvety red evening gown. She was sitting on a zebra, staring blankly at the camera with her mouth hanging open. I think it was a tampon ad.

"Nothing in her eyes," I said. "They're just dull. Dull and empty."

"Oof, yeah," Jelson agreed. "Zombie city. And she's got total blow-job mouth."

"What?"

"You know, that face all female models have, where they're sort of gasping, and their lips are parted kind of expectantly. They look ready for the reader's penis to just fly at their face at any second," Jelson explained. "It's totally a thing."

I started flipping through pages at random.

"Oh my God, you're totally right," I said. "Conditioner ad, blow-job mouth. Perfume ad, blow-job mouth. Bikini ad, blow-job mouth. Ugh, she looks like she's about to inhale about a gallon of salt water. Why would this make a straight woman want to buy things?"

Jelson shrugged.

"What would make an intelligent woman want to read this magazine at all?" he asked pointedly. I ignored him with great dignity.

"Jelson!" came a voice from across the courtyard. Amy Telenky was jogging over, looking freckled and bosomy in a tight tank top. Amy was formerly head cheerleader, but had to leave the squad last year because of some sprained tendon thing. Her decreased visibility at sports games and considerable weight gain got her all in a tizzy about lost popularity. She's been warding off loser status through the strategic deployment of her ever-increasing cleavage.

"Hey, Amy," said Jelson, closing his book but keeping his finger in it to hold his place.

"Hi, Amy," I said loudly.

"Hey, Allie," said Amy vaguely, not taking her eyes off Jelson. "Um, so, Jelson, I was wondering if you were going to Ronnie Ackersim's party on Friday?"

"Probably, yeah," said Jelson. "Isn't everybody going?"

Amy giggled like Jelson had made a joke. Girls do that around him when he's a guy. Then they ignore her actual jokes when she's a girl.

"Yeah, totally. Um, I was just wondering if you knew if you were going to be a boy or a girl on Friday?" said Amy.

"It's kind of hard to say," said Jelson, shrugging, smiling mildly. "I mean, do you know what pants you'll be wearing on Friday?"

Amy giggled some more.

"Oh, if I told you, you'd definitely come as a boy," she said, giving her hair a little toss.

"Right. Ha ha," said Jelson, rolling his eyes a little, but in a playful way. "Anyway, I'll probably be a boy. Ronnie and Pete are bringing drinks, right? I can drink more when I'm a guy without making a fool of myself."

"Cool," said Amy. "Well, I just wanted to pass along an invitation, in case you hadn't heard yet. I'll see you in gym."

She waved and walked away.

"No, Amy, I don't think I can make it, thanks for asking," I said pleasantly.

"You're not going?" Jelson asked.

"Hell no," I said. "Especially if you're gonna be a guy. At least if you're a girl I can tag along while you gossip about drama club with Lauren and Nikki. If you're a boy you're gonna run off and do keg stands with Ronnie and try to pee on tree frogs or whatever."

"Don't mock the tragedy of American boyhood," said Jelson, standing up and stretching. He was wearing dark jeans and a plain black T-shirt. He wriggled his bare toes on the warm cement of the courtyard. "We binge drink and wet ourselves 'cause we're scared to hug each other."

"Truly, I weep for you," I said, yawning and scratching my stomach.

"But seriously, you're totally welcome to come hang out with Ronnie and the guys. They won't be total dicks if I'm around, I promise."

"Believe me, I'm not worried about getting felt up." I waved a hand to indicate my sturdy log of a woman's body.

"I don't just mean like that," said Jelson. "I mean we can hang out. They'll be cool."

"I really don't feel like listening to everybody talk about what teachers they want to bone. Or who they've boned on the swim team. Or what it would be like to bone girls from the swim team and the lacrosse team at the same time."

"All right, all right, if it's really that big a deal, I'll go as a girl."

As if to emphasize her point, Jelson suddenly switched. Like I said, Jelson's change-ups aren't extreme. There's this kind of weird, fleshy ripple that travels along her body, but by the time you notice it, she's already done. Suddenly her jeans fit a little more snugly over her butt, the curve of her chin got a little softer, and the hand that moved to brush the hair from her eyes moved just a little more gently.

"What are you gonna tell Amy?" I asked. "You practically promised her a night of tipsy, testosterone-fueled groping."

"Please, I promised nothing." Jelson plonked her hands indignantly on her hips. Like I said, she keeps the same slim-hipped frame when she switches, but everything about the way she moves changes. She cocked her hips to one side, and, though small, they stuck out like a shelf. Maybe it was unintentional, but I could definitely read promises there.

I try not to be jealous of Jelson's attractiveness. I'm her best friend, so I see firsthand that while being pretty is definitely an asset, especially for a high school Swop, it's usually way more annoying than fun. But sometimes I look and can't help hating my own body. Both of Jelson's bodies seem to combine all that's cool about different genders. Meanwhile, I look like a chubby lesbian truck driver on my good days, and a potbellied, beer-guzzling retired linebacker on my bad days. If Jelson's everything that's best about male and female, I'm everything that's worst. I'm too square and thick and hulking to be a pretty girl, too soft and fleshy and floppy to be sexy like a man. It isn't easy.

"I'll just tell Amy I didn't feel like switching back after play practice." Jelson shrugged. "She'll cry about how I'll never see how much she cares about me, make out with Danny Everson instead, cry about how it's so sad they'll never get back together, and get over it."

I sighed. Doomed to be Jelson's unattractive androgynous sidekick for another weekend.

"Okay, I'll come. But I'm gonna be really weird and surly and make everyone question why you're friends with me."

Jelson smiled triumphantly as the bell rang for next period. She slipped her sandals on and turned to head back inside.

"Allie, darling, I wouldn't have it any other way," she said as she walked away, hips swinging like a pendulum.

❖

Drama club ran long on Friday. You could tell most of the kids were itching to go home and get ready for the party, but Mr. Niddio is nothing if not a big gay perfectionist, so we were stuck. Jelson's the performer. I'd rather stand in a pool of boiling oil than a spotlight, so I do lighting and tech.

Jelson is totally our drama star this year, and you can tell that Mr. Niddio practically fell over and died of happiness when Manetow High's own sexy Swop was revealed to be a talented thespian. He immediately announced a production of Shakespeare's *Twelfth Night*, and—surprise, surprise—cast Jelson as Viola, the girl disguised as a boy that everyone in the play falls madly in love with. The whole club is pretty sure we're doomed to put on *As You Like It*, *The Two Gentlemen of Verona*, and every one of the Bard's cross-dressing comedies before Jelson graduates. We'd do the cross-dressing tragedies too, but the PTA forbids the use of fake blood.

Not that I mind Shakespeare. Better *Twelfth Night* than *Bye Bye Birdie* or some Andrew Lloyd Webber disaster. Even if the high school acting is a catastrophe, the poetry is nice. Plus the play is all about fine dukes and ladies, so you get to see your classmates prance around in big ruffs and bright tights and funny short pantaloons. And with Mr. Niddio in charge you can guarantee that the tights will be very bright and the pantaloons as hilarious as possible. I think he uses wardrobe choices to work out some kind of latent childhood resentment toward high school students.

Late Friday afternoon found me sitting sleepily in the back row of the auditorium, watching Mr. Niddio try to shepherd a bunch of actors through a complicated bustling courtroom scene. The only problem with *Twelfth Night* is that it doesn't have a whole bunch of roles, so Niddio has to stick everybody into ensemble parts as sailors and castle guards and ladies-in-waiting and then give them something to do. I was technically supposed to be in the lighting booth, but Nikki Rofa had kicked me out so she could flirt awkwardly with Greg Hammelstein.

I was just nodding off when Keith Lamar, our one black kid, plopped down next to me.

"Hey, Keith," I said. Keith is another one of the drama club's best performers. He got cast as Duke Orsino, the hot royal man Viola marries at the end. He and Jelson have to kiss a whole bunch, and it is basically the most beautiful thing you have ever seen.

"Hey, Allie." Keith tugged angrily at his ruff. "Do you think I can take this off yet? We were supposed to finish like twenty minutes ago."

I shrugged.

"Dunno. Niddio has made everybody run this bit about five times, and he still isn't happy. Who knows when we'll get to leave?" I waved at Jelson, who was peeking around the curtain, squinting at the stage action and waiting for her cue. Or his cue. I couldn't actually tell. Jelson waved back and immediately got yelled at by Mr. Niddio and everyone had to start over.

"Stupid Jelson is the only one these outfits look good on," muttered Keith. I had to admit that he was right. Everyone else looked like paunchy Renaissance Faire rejects, while Jelson looked like something out of Britain's National Portrait Gallery.

"Poor kid got totally typecast," I said gravely.

"True fact," said Keith, now yanking fitfully at his tights. "But better her than me. When Niddio said we were doing Shakespeare, I can't even tell you how afraid I was we were gonna do *Othello*."

"That would have been so awkward for everyone involved."

"Tell me about it."

"I was hoping for *Rocky Horror*," said Tony Peluzzi, our one gay boy, as he sidled up behind us, sipping a ginger ale. Tony was playing Sebastian, Viola's twin brother. Everyone in the play falls madly in love with him too. Tony and Jelson don't actually look anything alike, but somehow, when they're acting on stage together, you would swear they sprang from the same womb. I don't pretend to understand it. Some kind of magical gay theater voodoo.

"I'm sure Niddio would let us do it, but it would never fly with the PTA," I said.

"Yeah, well, the PTA are a bunch of censorship-happy buzzkills," said Keith.

We chuckled, earning a dark look from Mr. Niddio that shut us up real fast.

"Are either of you guys in this next scene?" I whispered. They shook their heads.

"No," said Tony in a hushed voice. "This is Jelson's big love speech, coming up. You know, the one that makes Olivia go gay for Viola."

"Yeah," said Keith. "I don't think she's actually gotten a chance to do it yet. It's like the most famous part of the play."

"God, tech week and we still haven't done a full run," Tony sighed. "Someone shoot me."

"Well, maybe if *someone* hadn't had so many hissy fits about not being allowed to wear glitter nail polish—"

"Excuse me? Maybe if *someone* could learn to pronounce 'forsooth'—"

I rolled my eyes, turning my attention back to the performers. The bustle of the ensemble was gone, and it was just Jelson and Lauren Sharp—Viola and Olivia—on stage. I was struck again by my inability to tell whether Jelson was a boy or a girl. I had assumed that Jelson would just be a girl when Viola was openly a girl, and a boy while she was supposed to be disguised, to make the act super convincing.

The lights were dimmed, and Jelson and Lauren had spotlights on them. Jelson's was slightly off-center, probably because Nikki and Greg were busy sucking face in the lighting booth, but it didn't matter. Jelson still commanded all the attention. Something in the arch of the back, or the graceful tilt of the head, made it impossible to look at anything else.

"*Your Lord does know my mind; I cannot love him,*" said Lauren. She said a bunch of other stuff too, but it was hard to pay attention. As she spoke, Jelson's face became pained, those delicate features forming a look of quiet wretchedness on behalf of the lord she loved. It was hard to listen to Lauren when I hated her so much for making Jelson look that way.

"*A gracious person, but yet I cannot love him. He might have took his answer long ago,*" Lauren finished.

"*If I did love you in my master's flame, with such a suffering, such a deadly life, in your denial I would find no sense,*" said Jelson. "*I would not understand it.*"

I had been sure that once Jelson spoke, I would know. The voice would give it away, boy or girl. And yet somehow, I still couldn't tell. Jelson made Viola's tones quaver a little. But was it the voice of an artless boy, speech made high and strained by passion? Or was it the voice of a determined girl, trying to speak low, with all the gravity she felt?

"Yo, she's a girl right now, right?" muttered Keith, shifting uncomfortably in his seat.

"No way," hissed Tony, a little too fiercely. "He's definitely a boy."

"*Why, what would you?*" demanded Lauren from the stage. Her face was blushing bright pink, which was weird because I didn't think she was that good an actress.

Jelson hesitated, hand at her throat. Or his throat. I felt my fingers clasp automatically at my own throat, and the skin there was flushed and hot. My heart was hammering hard in my chest. Jelson looked uncertain, that fluid body poised and still. Somehow, tension seemed to gather in the air of the theater.

"*Make me a willow cabin at your gate, and call upon my soul within the house,*" said Jelson, eyes closed, body shaking slightly now. The voice, though—the voice was clear and sweet and sure. Too low for a girl, too high for a boy, it was a harmony of man and woman. "*Write loyal cantons of contemnèd love and sing them loud even in the dead of night; halloo your name to the reverberate hills and make the babbling gossip of the air cry out 'Olivia!'*"

Lauren's eyes were wide and awed, her mouth hanging slightly open. She looked like a prime example of blow-job mouth.

Jelson turned to her now, and gave a wry, tragic little smile.

"*O, you should not rest between the elements of air and earth, but you should pity me.*"

Lauren stared at Jelson when the speech was done, throat working convulsively.

"Line?!" she squeaked desperately.

She got a loud honk from Mr. Niddio in response as he blew his nose into his sleeve.

"I think that's enough for today, everyone," he said, shooing us away. "Everyone pack up and go home."

"You would think the famous speech would be a little longer," said Keith, unbuttoning his doublet.

"I know, right?" said Tony. "What's a canton?"

"Shut up," I said, a little too loudly. There was a vicious twinge happening deep in my belly, making me painfully nauseous.

"You okay, Allie?" asked Tony. "You look like you're gonna throw up."

"Uh, yeah, no, I'm fine." Jelson had spotted us and was bounding up the aisle toward us. Bounding like some kind of stupid, delicate, beautiful deer. My stomach clenched and I jerked up out of my seat. "No, actually, I gotta go," I said, shooting toward the exit. "Gonna barf. I'll see you guys later."

❖

Jelson picked me up for the party, since she'd gotten permission to use her mom's car. She was definitely, most emphatically, a girl when I got in the car. She had on a short skirt and high boots and had clearly just shaved her legs. Not that those things make you a girl, but they do make you kind of a more definite, emphatic girl. Right?

"Hey," she said. "You feeling okay? Keith and Tony said you almost yakked all over the theater today."

"Yeah, I'm fine." I slumped down in my seat. "I think it was just, like, PMS, y'know? Cramps."

"I thought you didn't usually get bad cramps," said Jelson, pulling the car onto the street.

"Yeah, well, sometimes they're shitty. Unexpectedly."

"I hear that," said Jelson.

"How would you know? Do you even get a period?"

"What? Yeah, I do, actually," said Jelson. "Just so you know."

"What, like, a normal one?" I asked, feeling grumpy and dull-witted.

"No. Not a normal one." Jelson frowned at the road. "Mine are really weird and awful and confusing, actually."

"Oh." I realized I had never thought about Jelson having to deal with the nasty bodily nitty-gritty of being a boy and a girl. Never thought about what puberty was like for her, or whether she could have kids, or if she worried about male pattern baldness and prostate cancer. I slumped even lower in my seat, feeling like a grade-A asshole.

We rode in silence for a few minutes, Jelson drumming her fingers distractedly on the steering wheel and me staring out the window and stewing about what an awful friend I am.

"Were you a boy or a girl today?" I blurted suddenly.

"What?" Jelson asked.

"At practice. When you were up on stage. You know, your big speech."

"Oh, the 'Cry out, Olivia!' speech?"

"Yeah."

Jelson shrugged. "I wanted to try something else for the part. Mr. Niddio said it was okay. He loved the idea, actually. So, I mean, I wasn't either. Not technically. Not physically. Or, I guess I was kind of both."

"What?" My belly did that painful, alien twinge again. "You—you can do that?"

"Yeah," said Jelson, sounding a little annoyed. "Of course I can. What do you think happens in between being a boy or a girl?"

"I—I mean I guess I never thought about it," I spluttered. And the truth was, I hadn't. But I was certainly thinking about it now, and the thought was painfully compelling. Jelson's long, slender body, hiding coyly under its clothes. Me, gently pulling those clothes off, seeing what that body looked like, touching it. Not a boy. Not a girl. Well, kind of like a boy, but also like a girl.

"What is wrong with you?" Jelson demanded.

I realized I had been breathing heavily. In a super-creepy way, through my mouth. I gulped.

"Nothing!" I almost shouted it.

"God, sorry I'm such an enormous, disgusting freak," Jelson said bitterly.

"What? What are you talking about?"

"Look at you, you're so grossed out you can't even stand to be near me."

"That's not—I didn't say that!" I yelled.

"Whatever. I would expect this from anyone else, Allie," said Jelson. "That's why I don't do it. Even when I want to stay in between, I don't let myself."

"What do you mean, 'when you want to'? Why would

you want to?" Even as I said it, I knew it was coming out completely wrong.

"Because I want to! Because it feels right. Because it feels like me. But I don't. I make myself go all one way or the other. Even if it feels wrong. Even if it hurts. Because I know how people feel about it."

She made an angry noise in her throat. "I just didn't think it would ever be an issue for you," she said, hands clenched tight on the steering wheel.

"I didn't say it was!" Desperation made my voice loud and shrill.

Jelson slammed on the brakes suddenly. I was jolted forward and almost strangled against my seat belt.

"We're here." She yanked up the parking brake. We were stopped behind a long line of cars, curving up the winding drive toward Ronnie Ackersim's house.

Jelson flounced out of the car and slammed the door behind her.

"Jelson! Jelson, wait!" I cried, struggling with the infuriating seat belt. I slipped on the gravel getting out of the car and skinned my knee. By the time I was up and huffing toward the house, Jelson had already disappeared inside.

"Goddammit," I muttered, pausing to catch my breath when I reached Ronnie's front steps.

Ronnie's family is one of the richest in town. They have the kind of big, ridiculous house that you have to believe his parents bought solely to live vicariously through their son's awesome high school parties. There's a giant, sloping lawn that you can comfortably puke on without bothering anyone. There are three stories of large, fashionably furnished rooms where you can sneak away and totally do it with somebody, or at least plausibly allege that you snuck away and totally did it with someone hot from out of town that no one else probably remembers. And they have a cool, cobblestone-paved back patio with dangly lanterns, a pool, and a killer sound system.

Ronnie's parties used to be a lot more exclusive, but Jelson convinced him they would produce more crazy stories if he let the whole grade attend. I think she loaned him a copy of *The Great Gatsby* and let him come to his own conclusions about it. I never really minded getting left out. Being at Ronnie's house too long makes me want to start a class revolution, and I have to guzzle some cheap beer and steal one of his karate trophies before the feeling goes away.

I could hear that, as usual, the action was on the back patio. I steeled myself and started making my way around the side of the house, trying to figure out what I would say to Jelson when I found her.

I almost ran smack into Amy Telenky and Danny Everson on my way. They were stuck awkwardly in the bushes, Danny pressing Amy against the side of the house, his fingers tugging urgently at the waist of her jeans.

"Come on, you said you wanted to get back together," said Danny.

"No, I said it would be nice if things were different," said Amy, trying to push him back.

"Uh, hey, Amy!" I called. "Nikki was looking for you!"

Danny pulled away and turned to scowl hideously at me. Amy shot to my side like a voluptuous heat-seeking missile.

"Oh my God, you're totally right!" She clamped her hand painfully on my upper arm. "I was totally supposed to do that thing for her! God, she must be so mad at me."

Amy strong-armed me away rapidly, leaving Danny to

mutter about dumb sluts and fat bitches and kick fitfully at the garden mulch.

"You okay?" I asked.

"Oh yeah," said Amy. "I mean, I don't think he actually would've done anything. He was just drunk. And, ugh, it's just so awkward, with guys. You know?"

"Uh, sure," I said. I was starting to lose feeling in my arm.

"Is Jelson here?" Amy asked tentatively.

"Yeah, she's somewhere. But she's a girl today."

"Oh." Amy's face fell. She sighed. "Well, I guess that's for the best. Do you want a daiquiri?"

"Is that like a margarita?" I asked suspiciously.

Amy laughed and led me to the bar on the back patio. I deposited her safely into the arms of Nikki and Lauren and about four Ashleys and an Ashleigh, and wandered away clutching a strong pomegranate mixed drink. My karma secure for the evening, I sat heavily in a pool chair and slurped my drink like it had done me wrong. I thought about running a hand up Jelson's thigh and shuddered a little.

I was interrupted by Keith plopping down next to me for the second time that day. I scowled at him in a way that I hoped came off as more antisocial than racist.

"Whatcha doin'?" he asked.

"Fetishizing my best friend's biology," I said darkly. "You?"

"Being drunk," he said. "And maybe a little gay."

"What?"

"Tony ran into me by the pool house. He was way drunker, even, than me. He was all like, 'Hey, we should rehearse our kiss for the play, it's so funny!'" Keith was talking about a pretty hot mistaken-identity kiss at the end of *Twelfth Night* that Mr. Niddio decided to sneak in. We're all eagerly awaiting the PTA fallout.

"That man is playing with you two like Barbie dolls," I said.

"Naw. Niddio's cool. Don't make him sound like a big creepo sexual predator. He said not to do it if it's more uncomfortable than funny."

"It is pretty funny," I admitted.

"Right? Right, gay dudes are funny. Even Tony admits it. Anyway, the thing is, when Tony said that, like, I think he was joking, but it got me, like, kind of hot, you know?"

"Are you telling me this because you think I'm a lesbian?" I accused.

"Yes," said Keith. "Anyway, I like girls, but it made me feel weird. I just wanted to tell someone." He stared wistfully at the shimmering lights on the surface of the pool.

"Right, well, I don't think it makes you gay or anything. We're young. I think we're all excited by the idea of anyone who might want to touch our penises."

"Sure, maybe." Keith sighed. "I hate this school."

"Me too."

"You want another drink?"

"No thanks."

"All right. Later, Allie."

"Bisexuality is a valid identity!" I called after him as he walked away. He gave me a thumbs-up over his shoulder. I sighed and stood, ready to wander back to the fun, awesome party.

People were dancing, but in this kind of shy, anemic way. Mostly boys and girls were separated, middle-school formal style. Boys were chilling out by the keg, girls by the bar, with only a few wary, horny ambassadors gyrating between the groups. My finished drink had left a sickly-sweet taste in my mouth, so I decided to sneak over to boy territory and nab a beer.

"I swear, Everson's upstairs right now, fuckin' Jelly," came Greg Hammelstein's voice as I approached the keg.

"Sick, dude, sick," said Ronnie, making a face. "I ran track with that kid."

"Which one?" asked Pete Deller, drunkenly.

"Uh, both, I guess." Ronnie sounded equally drunk. "Whatever. Gross. Jel's, like, like a guy."

"Pretty hot, though," said Greg, taking a swig of beer. "Hot chick, I mean," he amended hastily. "Like, she's hot when she's a chick. Kind of."

"Yeah, but think about it," said Pete. "What if, like, you were fuckin' him—her, I mean. Like, you were gettin' down to it, and he switched. Like, in the middle of it?"

"Aw, *sick!*" cried Ronnie and Greg, flinching visibly.

"Those Swops seriously freak me out," said Greg. "Right?"

"Totally," said Pete. Ronnie took a sip of beer and said nothing.

"Idiots," I muttered, deciding the beer was not worth it.

"You say something?" Pete demanded, turning around.

"Yeah, I said you're an idiot," I repeated loudly.

"Fuck off," said Pete. "Who invited you, bull dyke?"

"Everyone's invited, Pete," Ronnie said evenly. I felt suddenly bad about the karate trophies. Even if none of them were first place.

"Fag!" said Pete.

"You're the fag!" cried Ronnie.

"Oh my God, fuck you guys," I said, walking away.

"Dyke!" Pete yelled. Something smacked me on the back of the head and I felt a cold trickle run down my neck. Pete, or one of his devoted groupies (no homo), had nailed me with a full cup of beer.

I wish I could say I ran back and punched Pete right in the face, taking a brave stand for ostracized gender-nonconforming kids everywhere. But actually, I just hunched my shoulders and kept walking, silently praying that Pete didn't have a brick handy. I was contemplating starting to walk home when I bumped right into Jelson.

"Dammit, Allie, watch where you're going!" She sounded flustered and furious.

"Sorry," I said forlornly.

She crossed her arms and scowled at me. She looked like she wanted to say something else angry, but couldn't think of anything. She sniffed.

"Why are you covered in beer?"

"Hate crime," I said. "Where have you been?"

"Upstairs. Danny said he wanted to ask me something about Amy."

"All the guys thought you two were getting it on," I said.

Jelson heaved a tired sigh. "No, Danny didn't get any. He sure tried, though."

"Are you okay? What happened?"

"I punched him in the goddamn mouth."

"You're so cool," I said wistfully.

Jelson shrugged. "It's not that impressive when you can dramatically increase your upper-body strength at will."

I looked closer at the arms crossed over Jelson's chest, squinting in the shadowy light of the patio, and saw that they were a little too thick for Jelson's girl arms. So were the thighs poking out from under Jelson's short skirt. I stared a little too long at the thighs.

"Is there a problem?" Jelson demanded. The voice had thrown me off. Well, the voice and the skirt and the pushup bra. It wasn't a boy's voice, because Jelson wasn't totally a boy. Jelson was in-between again.

"Guh," I said.

"Oh my God, I don't need this." Jelson started to walk away.

"Jelson, wait!" I moved to follow. "I'm sorry!"

"Leave me alone!"

"No, I need to talk to you!" I grabbed Jelson's shoulder, wanting her to look at me.

"You have no idea what it's like!" Jelson threw me off, obviously fighting back tears. "You're so secure, being the way you are. You're totally okay being in-between, you don't care what anyone thinks."

"What?" I said, thrown off-guard. "Jelson, what are you talking about?"

"You strut around, big tough macho butch girl, and you don't let anybody change you. You don't let anyone push you back and forth." Jelson's tears were smearing his mascara. "You're everything that's best about boys and girls, together. You're so strong, and so kind." Jelson's shoulders shook.

"Jelson," I said, my heart beating hard.

"And I know how you look at me! You laugh at me, the way I am with boys, and the way I am with girls. You think it's so stupid!"

"Jelson, I don't think you're stupid—"

"I only do it because I'm scared," said Jelson. "I don't know how else to be!"

"Jelson, I had no idea you felt like that," I said. "You're just so good at it, so good at being a boy or a girl, it always seemed so natural."

"Oh, please." Jelson laughed harshly. "There is nothing natural about this outfit."

"Okay, yeah, totally fair." I smiled weakly. "But I always felt so gross next to you. So lumbering and awkward."

"Oh my God, Allie, have you looked in the mirror?" Jelson put a hand on my face. I made a horrible little noise.

"Are you all right?"

"No!" I reached out, put an arm around Jelson's waist, and pulled us close together. I gasped, feeling the hard, soft warmth of that body. Of Jelson. My best friend.

And then we were two freaky, androgynous high school queers, kissing in the dark on some rich kid's patio. Jelson is my best friend. I love Jelson.

THE TEA BOWL
JUSTINE F. LANE

The first time I saw her, she was standing in the doorway of the English staffroom where I had a desk. It was mid-January, the coldest time of year in Japan. Aside from the gas heater, I was alone. She looked at me and asked where my supervisor was. Many of the final-year students had been coming to see him for last-minute help as they prepared for their university entrance exams. I called him, then lowered my eyes back to my language studies.

But she kept her attention on me, and as I looked up, she spoke to me in slow, steady English. "I heard that you're a vegetarian," she said. I was surprised, not because she knew—I'd told many students, and word spreads quickly. And then there was that rather graphic animal rights board I'd put up in the corridor. What surprised me was that she'd brought it up. No other student had before.

"Yes," I replied, "that's right." At this, she grinned broadly, poking her head a little farther into the office.

"Me too," she said. I stared at her, taken aback. I'd never met a vegetarian student here. I told her as much. She smiled some more, then stepped across the threshold. Her expression turned to one of great concentration as she struggled to find the

English words she wanted to say. "Since I was a child," she said. "I never liked meat."

I told her I thought that was great, and really meant it. Then my supervisor came to fetch her, and our conversation ended.

The next day, again, I was at my desk when the door to the staffroom slid open. It was a heavy door and always made a sound when it was opened or closed. I looked up to see the same student. She smiled and gave a small wave. Again, she asked for my supervisor. This time, he was at his desk. As she walked past me toward him, I looked at her hair. It was thick, jet black and straight, and cut short, above the ears. It was bordering on a bowl cut, but cute. I looked at her clothes. She was wearing a plaid flannel shirt, in the '90s farm style that had recently returned to popularity. The collar was open, and I could see the neck of her white T-shirt. She wore some kind of cargo pants and a bright orange hoodie. Suspicious, I thought, then checked myself. I returned my concentration to my studies, but the new grammar point didn't make sense, and my chest felt strange. It was burning, right in the center. My palms were getting kind of sweaty, too. I wondered whether the pickles I'd eaten with lunch had been okay. Or perhaps I was getting a cold—there were lots going around.

About twenty minutes later, she walked past my desk again on her way out. She paused and looked at me.

"I heard that you're originally from Africa," she said.

I was at least a head taller than her, but since I was sitting, I was forced to look up at her face. It was oval-shaped and very soft. The strange feeling in my chest intensified and my throat felt like it was closing as I confirmed my nationality. "That's great," she said, grinning. She had nice teeth, I thought, and then wondered at the randomness of that cogitation. I usually didn't notice people's teeth unless there was something strange about them, or they had none at all.

She asked if I knew Swahili at all. I shook my head. She told me that she wanted to study it at university. I was impressed. I asked her why she wanted to study it. "I want to go to Africa and help the people there," she said sincerely. Despite the simplicity of this statement and the problematic elements to it, I couldn't help but marvel at how cool she was. I didn't usually admire people I'd just met—I preferred to judge them savagely.

After she had left, the strange feeling in my chest persisted. I felt hot, and my heart was beating fast, pumping sweat out of my pores. What was going on? Fifteeen minutes went by, and I had just decided to go to the sick room when my supervisor walked by. Without thinking, I blurted out that the student was vegetarian. He was confused.

"Which one?"

"Er, the one that was in here just now," I said. But two more girls had come to see him since. He gave me some names. But I didn't know hers. "The one with the short hair," I tried, my heart pounding. Comprehension spread across his face.

"Ah, you mean her!" he said. "She's vegetarian? I had no idea." I repeated her name as he had said it, my clumsy foreign tongue struggling to get the right pronunciation.

He corrected me a couple of times, then said, "It's quite an unusual name—it means 'child of the wind.'" I imagined leaves and pink blossom petals gently blowing across a late-spring landscape.

My supervisor was still talking. "I don't know the exact details, but she lives alone with her mother," he said. "They're—how do you say it—pottery?"

I giggled. "Potters?"

"Yes—potters. Every month they sell their goods at a temple market."

Her "cool" points instantly doubled. In this society that was dominated by paper-shuffling "salarymen" and "office ladies," a humble, creative, and independent trade like pottery was something that earned my respect.

The next day, I was feeling much better—no more chest burning, perspiration, or palpitations. I chalked up the previous day's ailment to heartburn and put on nice clothes for a change: pinstripe pants, a collared shirt, and a black V-neck pullover. At work, I decided to finish sticking up some posters before doing anything else. As I was balanced on a desk, pre-cut strips of tape all over my hands, I heard the door to the staffroom slide open. My heart started pounding again. A boy's voice called for my supervisor, and I relaxed. Then the door slid open again. This time, a familiar voice, deep but feminine, called for my supervisor. In an instant, all the feelings were back. My legs trembling, I leapt off the desk, ripping the crotch of my pants on the way down. As the threads snapped, suddenly I understood what was going on. I opened the classroom door to see her beautiful, young face, and it was clear that I had fallen for it.

Crap, I thought. I did mention the fact that she was a student, right? And that I was an English teacher? As my supervisor led her to his desk, I returned to my own and had a discreet freak-out. Oh my God! How could this have happened? And so quickly? And why? I was in a relationship. I'd come to Japan with my partner, and our anniversary was coming up. But no matter how sternly I talked to myself, I couldn't think my way out of it. This girl was having a physical effect on me like nothing I'd ever experienced. It felt like she was holding a white-hot poker to my breastplate, but I couldn't—or rather, didn't want to move away from it.

I had to speak to her some more. I devised a smooth strategy to snare her on her way out. It felt like she had been talking to my supervisor for hours when she finally passed by my desk. "Hey…" I mangled her name. She stopped to look at me. Remembering my ripped pants, I clamped my thighs shut. How long had I been sitting with my legs flapping open like that? "I heard that your parents make pottery," I said, using her way of speaking. She smiled, glancing at my supervisor.

"Yes, it's the family business," she said. She seemed pleased, but puzzled, that I was interested.

"That's cool!" I said. "What kind of pottery do you make?" She told me that it was a traditional style, using simple blue and white designs. It sounded great. All was going according to plan. "Well, er, do you have any tea bowls?" I asked. For a second, she didn't understand. I repeated the word in Japanese, probably inadvertently swearing at her. She smiled and said that they had the bowls. "Well, I'd like to buy one," I said. "For tea ceremony. I, er, study it, actually." I really was studying Japanese tea ceremony, but had yet to purchase any bowls.

"Then I'll bring you one," she said, without hesitation.

"Great, just tell me how much it is," I said.

"No, no," she said, looking confused. "I'll give you one, as a present."

I was blown away. Tea bowls cost thousands of yen. And apparently her family wasn't well-off; yet here she was, a student I'd only spoken to once or twice, saying she'd give me one. I couldn't accept it. We argued about it politely for a minute, but in the end she won. She brought her hands close to my desk and tried to explain about the different sizes of bowls they had. Although her English was fine, I couldn't make sense of what she was saying. I was captivated by her hands. They were so small, so cute. Her nails were very short—again, suspicious, I thought. I drifted off into a fantasy involving those hands and the warm, moist places they'd fit into so perfectly. When she stopped speaking, I jolted back to reality, nodding and reassuring her that the size was perfect. I could have been agreeing to a thimble for all I knew. Then she was gone.

I wondered how old she was. She had to be at least eighteen, turning nineteen. That was the average age for the final-year students. I sucked my teeth. It was only a three-year age difference. I'd dated a girl eight years older than me, and that had worked…well, sort of. Okay, not at all, but it wasn't because of the age difference. But what was I thinking? I was in a relationship. Yes, these feelings were strong. Every cell in my body was filled with a longing that felt eons old. She'd be graduating in just six weeks, and then a relationship would no longer be forbidden. But it was a ridiculous idea. What was I going to do, break up with my girlfriend and run off with a teenager? Open up our relationship like we'd talked about doing at some point? Have an illicit but steamy affair in a broom closet or love hotel somewhere? Preposterous. Yet, cruelly, I allowed myself to see a possibility.

That evening at home, I felt compelled to tell my partner at least part of what I was going through. Writer types are always oversharing. "So," I cleared my throat, "I'm getting a new tea bowl." She didn't look up from the scrapbook she was pasting stuff into.

"That's great," she said, a pre-programmed response.

I added, "From a student. She's a vegetarian too, can you believe it?" I was hoping and fearing she would pick up on what I was really trying to say. But she merely glanced up and said, "That's nice." I couldn't contain myself.

"I know, isn't it?" I exclaimed, beaming, and proceeded to tell her the whole story, minus the part where I fell in love. She didn't seem to find anything about it suspicious, and she even said she'd sew my pants, if I paid her. That's how it was with her—nothing for free.

I was burdened by the detail I hadn't told my girlfriend, but I just didn't have the guts to do it. I didn't know how she would react, and as much as I wanted to tell her, I didn't want to hurt her. I had no appetite for dinner, but ate so as to avoid suspicion. We usually went to bed around ten, but I stayed up well past midnight, sitting alone in the small lounge and letting the invigorating, but unstable, surging energy of love carry me into imaginary lands where I chased the child of the wind through wheat fields and laughed in her bare, sun-kissed arms, completely carefree and absorbed in the moment.

From the next day, I waited. I had no idea when the tea bowl would arrive. She'd asked me when I would next be at school, and stupidly, I'd said I would be there every day. Even though I had a quiet schedule for the next couple of weeks, I was chained to my desk until she returned. Every time the door slid open, I palpitated and perspired. I made a mix CD of music I liked, since she'd mentioned she was into rock music and was learning guitar. I wrote out the track list for the mix CD in blue pen and added a few doodles, and, after some thought, my e-mail address. I folded it up and put it inside the CD case.

I paid close attention to the floor by the doorway. Students normally wore standard-issue green and white canvas school slippers, but once they'd left the school, as the final-years had, they wore the gray slippers used for guests when they came to see teachers. Our staffroom was a no-slipper zone, which meant you had to take them off and leave them outside. Every time I came back from the toilet and saw a pair of those gray slippers outside the door, I almost fainted.

To channel my gushing emotions, I took to writing haiku. Here is one of them:

Calm winter morning
Seeing me, she smiles and then—
A storm breaks inside.

Not exactly Matsuo Basho, I know.

I went through two weeks of waiting, each day growing more and more frustrated. I studied Japanese with fervor, breezing through the grammar and practicing lines I thought might come in useful in the future, like, *"Watashi wa kimi no ha ga suki."* That means "I like your teeth."

There was a brief respite at the graduation ceremony. As I took my place with the other foreign teachers, along the side of the gymnasium, I scanned the final-years for her. They were all up at the front, arranged in their homeroom classes. I was wearing glasses, which were deliberately a couple of prescriptions too weak while I tried to strengthen my eyes through exercise and rose water. So I had to tilt the frames diagonally to see the faces of the kids up front. Eventually I found her. She was standing in one of the back rows, wearing a black suit with a white collared shirt, the top buttons open. Most of the other girls wore expensive kimonos with fruit and flower decorations. I focused on her, peering through my skewed glasses for the entire ceremony.

As they filed out to tears, applause, and congratulations, I waited for her. As she passed me, I clapped extra loud. But she didn't see me.

She finally came to the staffroom again on the day of the school festival. I was actually busy that day and wasn't expecting her. I'd put on a three-piece suit for the occasion, so at least I looked decent—some might even say dashing. When I got to school, she was already there. She was wearing the flannel shirt and orange hoodie again. I wondered if she knew how lesbionic she looked, or if she even was gay. Some of the dykiest women I'd ever seen here were also some of the straightest.

We chatted a little about her entrance exams and her plans to buy a laptop for university. I was flustered, but tried to seem cool. I said "cool" so many times that she picked it up too and by the end of the conversation, she was even dropping it in. I gave her the mix CD. I'd been keeping it in my top drawer, anally checking that it was still there, twice a day. Just in case a snake carried it off or something.

When I gave it to her, she seemed really happy. She grinned more broadly than usual and opened the CD in front of me. I apologized for my bad handwriting, some of which was a scrawled attempt at Japanese, but she looked at me seriously, her eyes dancing, and said, "It's beautiful." I thought I would melt into a puddle on the floor.

She went into the adjacent room to fetch her bag, a black rucksack, and returned also carrying a small paper bag. It had some strange Engrish writing about animals on it. She hesitantly held it out, saying that she hoped it was all right. I thanked her profusely and then noticed the time. I had to moderate one of the festival debates, which would be starting in five minutes. The tea bowl would have to wait, but I was silently grateful for an exit excuse. I didn't know how long I could have stayed composed, standing so close to her.

Waiting in the library for the debate to start, my heart felt like it was going to beat right out of my chest and leave me collapsed and bleeding on the floor. But I felt more alive than I had in many months. A roaring sound, like that of waves crashing on rocks at high tide, filled my ears. No one else seemed to hear it. I fought to regain some semblance of sanity and stability. I wanted to run up to the debate stage and tell the audience that my tea bowl had arrived. Instead, I sat down and focused on the clock behind the debaters, allowing myself to become absorbed in its ticking.

The debate was only an hour, but by my watch, it was an eternity. When it was eventually over, I went back to the staffroom and opened the packet. Inside was a thick cardboard box. I lifted it out, took off the lid, and carefully parted the protective tissue paper. Inside was the most beautiful handcrafted tea bowl. The upper half of the outside was a delicate white, with pictures of hares and tufty grass painted in blue around the outside. The inside was a swirling sky blue. The base was unpolished clay, which complemented the blue. It was like holding the sky and earth in the palm of your hand.

Also in the box was a small, polished shard of pottery with a blue pattern on it, and the kanji for her name. It was one of her bowls—she had made it herself with those small, strong hands. It was the best present I had ever received. I carried it home gingerly, and showed it off to my girlfriend.

It was then that she began to suspect something. The more I rambled on about the student, the lower her brows sank. When she eventually spoke, there was sadness and hurt in her eyes.

"So what you're trying to say to me, is that you like this girl?" she asked. I sighed and confessed the whole truth. I could sense emotions brimming in her, but she kept cool and chose to repeat just one sentence: "Nothing can happen." She said it would all pass with time. I wasn't so sure, but I didn't say that. The thought of not seeing her again was not one I could accept. My heart was heavy as I told her I at least wanted to become friends with the girl. My partner looked at me levelly, took my hand, and nodded.

The mixture of guilt, longing, and electric excitement flipped my insides out and, suddenly exhausted, I sank onto the bed. I apologized. I had not intended any of this to happen.

At school the next day, I wrote a thank-you note for the tea bowl. I asked another teacher to translate some phrases into natural Japanese for me. She was suspicious, but said nothing. "I'd like to treat you to dinner," was not standard textbook stuff. But the wind girl had expressed interest in a guidebook to vegetarian restaurants in Japan I had, so I was going to lend it to her. I wrote that it was unfair to not do something in return for such a beautiful tea bowl, so, if she liked, I would buy her lunch at one of the restaurants sometime.

The next time she came in, I gave her the book. Waiting for her reply, I could hardly eat or sleep. I'd told her not to rush— she could return the book any time before spring vacation, I'd said. Even though I had no more classes, I kept coming to school, to wait for her. I berated myself for wasting time at work. It was cherry blossom season. I should be frolicking in the park, I thought.

In the last few days before the holidays officially started, she came to school for the last time. The heavy door to the staffroom slid open and she stepped inside, holding a bag of guitar books. She wanted to return these to my supervisor. But he wasn't in. She said she'd come back later. She took my guidebook out of the bag and handed it to me, flipping open the cover to reveal her note back to me. Then she left.

My heart was thumping and my hands quivering as I unfolded the note. I felt like my body would burst, I had so much loving energy for her. I smelled the paper and traced her handwriting, imagining her writing it. The note said thanks for the book and the CD. She said she would e-mail me once she'd bought a laptop, to tell me which tracks she liked best. I checked both sides of the paper. But it didn't say anything about my offer. My heart sank into the depths of my chest.

A few weeks later, as she had said she would, she e-mailed me. Her message didn't say much. She thanked me for my kindness and told me which songs she liked on the CD. She used cute, simple, clear English, which only endeared her more to my heart.

I replied immediately, on the train back from a daytrip. I told her about the trip and wished her well, not expecting any further communication. To my surprise, my phone vibrated not even an hour later with her reply. She said that her hometown was near the area I'd visited and asked me one or two general questions. Encouraged by the communication, I sent a lengthy reply, asking her about her hometown, and why she'd chosen the name of a long-dead, famous artist for her e-mail address.

She never replied.

Months later, she e-mailed to ask if I was still working at the school. She told me what her name meant in Swahili. I sent a short, polite reply. It was time to let go. I couldn't keep stoking this fire indefinitely. She would never take me up on my dinner offer. I didn't know if she would ever date women. She might even have already been dating a woman.

I don't know if she had any idea what I felt, but I want to

believe she had some notion. She was like another manifestation of my own soul, flowing gently through the universe. She opened up something inside me. The love that had raged for her had quieted, but it tore through some of my assumptions and ideas on its course, forging a new path forward. For one thing, I now understood why some people had affairs, or advocated polyamorous relationships.

I had been in love before; indeed, I still was, with my partner. But for the first time in my life, I really knew what it meant to fall in love; physically, unexpectedly, and with all of oneself. It's a force more powerful than logic or social obligations. It turned me on my head and held me captive like a dominatrix, giving me pain and pleasure, but no safeword to stop the act from playing out.

I also know that if that girl, the child of the wind, was ever to come into my life again, I would fall right back into those feelings. No matter who I was with or where I was—if she made a move, I don't know if I would be able to refuse. The weight of these words keeps me from uttering them. It's a truth that I simultaneously hope and fear someday having to face.

Though I often use the tea bowl she gave me, I never drink out of it myself.

THE PIANO PLAYER
THOMAS GRAZIANO

There was something about piano music that made me want to fall in love. The eloquent notes touched more than just my eardrums; I felt a connection to its rhythmic beauty that I had never felt to any other type of music. The sweet notes drifted through the air, sending images to my mind of flowery fields, kisses, and general happiness. That was one great thing about music, to my mind—it wasn't just auditory, but visual as well. Some songs are just so beautiful you have to conjure images to go along with it. And it sure didn't hurt when a cute boy was the one playing the piano.

Except when it was at your grandma's funeral.

It seemed like the only time my entire family got together was for a funeral. Not for someone's birthday, or even Christmas. But a fucking funeral. Goes to show how much we all loved each other.

I was sitting in the last row, weeping like everyone else. I wasn't looking at anyone and wasn't even listening to the pastor's speech. Just thinking about the memories and crying. No more hugs from my grandma, no more of her amazing homemade ice cream sundaes, no more of her genuine love.

After the speech, a small piano performance was held to honor her favorite songs. As soon as the notes drifted through the air, I recognized the song. My grandma had heard it in some movie and had fallen in love with it. She would listen to this song while she cooked, while we played card games, while we would get ready for bed. I never got sick and tired of the song; it was just that beautiful. Midway through, I finally looked up for the first time. The boy who was playing it had his eyes closed, his body moving along with the music. He was young, my age, and had a swirl of blond hair that seemed so bold against his black sweater. I wanted to see his eyes, but they remained closed as he played the song with ease. He didn't make any mistakes; it was as if his hands belonged to a professional with years of experience. My grandma would've been happy to see that we found someone as passionate for the song as she had been.

❖

A week later, I was walking through my college campus when I spotted him alone in a single piano room. That's the benefit (and curse, some would say) of going to a tiny school—you run into anyone and everyone eventually. His hands moved swiftly across the board; his body moved gently with the melody of the song. His eyes were closed, which was good since that meant he wouldn't be able to see me drooling over him.

This had happened before. I'd spot a cute boy and then my wishful thinking would take total control over my mind. I wasn't desperate on a superficial level—I was just desperate because I was a gay college student who had never even had his first kiss. But it's the romantics that always get hurt in the end, isn't it? They envision such a lush life with the perfect soul mate, which is ultimately destroyed by a little thing called reality.

But at that moment, I just wanted to admire him. He opened his eyes and his hands stilled over the keys. And then, without even looking at me, he asked, "Do you want to come in and listen?"

If this had happened in high school, I would've been too nervous to even talk to him and would be already fleeing to class. But in college, I'd learned that sometimes you needed to make your own miracles happen.

So I said yes and sat down beside the piano. Notes filled the air as his fingers struck key after key after key. He struck a few deep dramatic notes with a ferocity one would expect to see in a football game. I couldn't help but smile in admiration.

When he was finished, I said, "Bravo, bravo."

He stood up and bowed. "Thank you, thank you." He extended his hand. "I'm Wesley."

I shook his hand. Despite striking the piano keys with such force, his hand was gentle and smooth. I didn't want to let go. "I'm Will."

He pointed to a bracelet on my wrist, made up of thread and a rainbow pattern of beads. "Cool bracelet."

"Thanks."

That bracelet was my key to finding a boy. Sometimes, it's really difficult to tell if a boy is gay or not. I remembered reading about how a boy's hair whorl direction reveals their sexuality, so during class, I would sit behind a cute boy and sketch the direction of his hair, and then go home and see if it matched the gay one or not. And then I'd slapped myself and promised not to be so stupid. But I really wanted a kiss. Really wanted a boy. So if a gay boy saw my rainbow bracelet, he would then know I was gay and that it was safe to pursue me. All my stars would align and I would finally meet my Prince Charming. That's how it always went in my head, anyway. I was cursed—or blessed—with a heart that was continually on the search for its match. I blamed the beating organ in my chest that took control over my brain and demanded to be fed with kisses and cuddling and love it had been deprived of for nineteen years.

His eyes twinkled. "So same time, same place tomorrow?"

I smiled. "That would be great."

Later that day, I went on a hike with my best friend Tiffany. She always relied on nature to help her get through tough times in life. With my grandma's recent passing, she decided that a hike would do me some good.

"He sounds wonderful," she said after I told her about Wesley. We had reached a point where we could overlook a deep valley, with trees stretching on for miles and miles beneath us. "Are you nervous about tomorrow?"

"I thought I would be. But I'm not. He didn't make me nervous like boys usually do."

She laughed. "That's a good sign. Little Will finally has a boyfriend!"

"Oh stop. He's not my boyfriend…yet. Hell, I don't even know if he's gay or not!"

"If he liked your rainbow bracelet, he's gay."

"I know, but I still need to find out for sure. I can't just ask him, 'Hey, do you like boys?'"

"Sure you can," she said. "And you're long overdue for a boyfriend."

"Tell me about it."

I thought once I entered college, I would find someone.

But every boy that I thought might just perhaps be gay turned out not to be. That was one good thing about social networking. You could stalk people and find out information about them without ever even talking to them in person. But as soon as I saw the word "straight" on their profiles, a long depression followed. Unfortunately, I couldn't find Wesley's profile. I could've sworn I heard the universe laughing at my misfortune.

"And will I be invited to the wedding?" Tiffany asked.

"Only if you promise to bring your signature homemade peanut butter cookies."

"Anything for you, Will. Anything."

"Hey, you know what I was thinking about? If I was straight, and you were straight, I'm pretty sure we'd be dating."

"And planning our wedding." She winked.

❖

The very next day, I practically ran to the piano room, where Wesley greeted me with "Hey, Will," and a perfect, flawless smile the likes of which I never thought I'd receive.

I sat down. "Someone seems excited today."

"I just love when someone is interested in my music."

He then began to play his own composition, a balance of a romantic melody and a sad one. My gaze shifted from his hands, floating over the piano keys with such precision and focus, to Wesley himself. He bit his lip with focus, clearly determined to not make a mistake. He never met my eyes; he was focused on the piano. But as the notes concluded in a mellow finale, his eyes finally met mine as his hands fell to his lap.

"That was a beautiful piece. When did you write it?" I asked.

"I was thirteen," he said. "I wanted to create a piece that would impact others the same way that other piano songs had impacted me. I wanted to provide an escape, a romantic escape."

"You did a great job. But it also had a sad tone to it."

"Romance isn't always happy."

I nodded. "In a way, sadness can be beautiful."

"And it's something everyone can relate to."

For the next few days, we met in the same room, where he would play song after song. Some songs he composed himself, others were from famous musicians. And I never got the chance to bring up any way of asking about his sexuality.

"You know which composers I like the most?" he asked one day. "Film composers. Their songs are just filled with so much emotion that's impossible to resist."

"You would make a great film composer. You have the passion for it."

"We'll see. It's such a long shot."

"Don't doubt yourself. You've already blown me away with all your original piano songs. Imagine what you could do with a full orchestra."

"Now, *that* would be cool." He smiled at me and for a brief moment, I wanted to lean in and kiss him, but he turned away before I could do anything.

Afterward, he gave me a few CDs of his favorite composers and songs. I listened to them before I fell asleep each night, some songs sad, some adventurous, and some mystical.

❖

"Can I ask you something?" A few days later, after he had just finished playing another round, we stood outside the piano building. Nighttime was quickly approaching—the sky had darkened, and a few stars were already visible through the tree branches above us. The campus seemed desolate and quiet, as if everyone had gone home.

"Sure, anything."

"What about you? What do you want to do with your life?"

"Help people, I guess. Through counseling or something."

He nodded. "You could do that. You're a great listener."

"And you're a great composer."

I was about to ask if he had a girlfriend or something, but he realized he was late for dinner with his family and hurried away. This would be about the seventh time I would have to report back to Tiffany and tell her that I was too chicken to ask him.

"Come on, Will! What happened to making your own miracles happen?" she said later. We sat on her bedroom floor, cutting out pictures from magazines for one of her class projects.

"I know, I know, *I know!*"

She pointed her scissors at me. "Obviously, you don't! We need to make sure our pact doesn't come true!"

We had made a pact earlier that year that if we didn't find the love of our lives by the time we were forty years old, we'd move to the gay capital of England, Brighton, and just live out our lives there. We needed somewhere that was very far away, and a place where English was the dominant language. So that gay beach town seemed like the best place to go.

And then one day, I hurried down the hall to the piano room, eager to arrive early. A piano melody wafted through the air, and I recognized the melody as my grandma's favorite song. My hands began to shake with anticipation as my chest swelled with emotion—nostalgia for my grandma's sweet smile as she listened to the music combined with my continuing fascination with Wesley. I arrived at the door, turned the knob slowly, and walked in unnoticed. His eyes were closed again. The notes wafted through the air, lighter than feathers. Each of his fingers struck each key with such careful precision, with just the right amount of force, and I couldn't help but admire it. This was what passion looked like.

"It's a beautiful song," he said.

"It was my grandma's favorite," I said. "Thanks for playing it at her funeral."

He looked up at me, where I could finally see his face in full detail. Light freckles were sprinkled along his cheeks. His eyes were blue with speckles of brown. His hair looked softer than my childhood teddy bear and just as dark.

"That was *your* grandma?"

I nodded. "Every time she listened to that song, she just seemed so happy. And it made me happy to see her like that. And that's how I feel when I listen to you play."

He leaned forward and kissed me. And I kissed back.

The excitement from his lips overwhelmed me. They were smoother than I ever imagined them to be. I touched his back, his arms, his face. He touched my arms, gentle yet strong. I never wanted to let go of that perfect moment. I felt like the luckiest guy in the world, for I was kissing a boy who had genuine kindness and love.

My wish had finally come true.

He then sat down and played the song again from the start.

I sat beside him, looking from his kind face to his graceful hands and up to his face again. I was in a dream, surely. A daydream, a night dream, just a dream.

Students strode by the room and saw us cuddling together. Some smiled and carried on with their day, while others gawked at us like we were animals locked in a zoo. Society seemed divided, but it didn't matter. I had a piano and I had a boy, and that was all I needed in that one moment.

And as I walked to class, I made a mental note to give Tiffany the honor of finally cutting off my bracelet.

CRYSTAL CRISIS
A.J. SLATER

Psst," Crystal whispered, trying to get Ryan's attention. "Ryan," she tried a second time. When her best friend finally picked up her bookmark, signaling she was out of her reverie, Crystal asked, "Can I borrow a pencil?"

"Sure." Ryan laughed at the familiarity of the scene. She was so used to it that she called it déjà vu. As usual, Crystal had yesterday's homework in front of her, rushing to get it done before their English teacher remembered to collect it. And usually adding to Crystal's daily chaos, it was a regular problem trying to find a working pencil.

"Cheerleading practice or Justin?" Ryan inquired while nodding toward the unfinished work. She handed over the spare writing implement she always kept in her backpack just for any kind of "Crystal Crisis."

"Both," Crystal grunted as she scribbled down half-thought-out answers. "He picked me up after practice and every time I tried to get out of his gigantic truck, he would find an excuse to call me back in."

Crystal had beautiful blond hair with highlights that made it shine, and she had sparkling blue eyes to match. She could have been a model if her heart desired, with her long legs and a toned body. Every teenage boy craved to get their hands on her. Crystal's most unique feature, however, was a small birthmark on the back of her neck that resembled a dove.

"Would any of these excuses have anything to do with his twenty-four-seven hard-on?" Ryan joked.

Crystal mimicked throwing up in her mouth and Ryan laughed out loud. This was the only part of her day when she felt at peace. The rest of the day she was habitually looking over her shoulder. As soon as she left the room, something awful was bound to happen—her books would be thrown to the floor, or she'd be slammed into the dirty, beige walls, or someone would trip her into a group of freshmen who knew enough about the pecking order to let her fall to the floor.

"Why do you date him if he grosses you out so much?" Ryan asked as Crystal finished the homework just in time to pass it to the front of the classroom.

Crystal shrugged nonchalantly. "Peer pressure. I'm the captain of the cheerleaders and he's the captain of the basketball team. Apparently we were made for each other." Crystal mocked her own words by adding air quotation marks with her fingers. "I'm so breaking up with him at the end of the season or when someone more adorable and smarter asks me out."

Ryan took a huge gulp. She was undoubtedly smarter than Justin, and Crystal was always telling her how adorable she was. *Is Crystal hinting at me? She couldn't be, could she?* Ryan quickly faced the front awkwardly. Crystal was her only friend, though if anyone knew it, they both would be slaughtered for interrupting the status quo. Ryan wouldn't ruin their relationship by hitting on her.

Nevertheless, she couldn't help but smile and blush at the thought. Crystal was her one and only high school crush.

The dream of them enjoying a night out at the movies or the bowling alley was one that Ryan welcomed.

"What the hell are you smiling about, you fag?"

"Justin, leave her alone, she's not bothering you."

Ryan heard Crystal come to her defense. She hadn't seen anything because she ducked her head as an automatic response to the sound of Justin's voice. This was how a horrible day always began. Some jock or popular girl would disturb Ryan's only time with Crystal. After that, the day wasn't even worth going through the motions for.

"She might not be bothering me, but Janna says she's bothering you," Justin said.

This is going to be bad, Ryan thought. *Real Bad.*

"I asked her for a pencil and she loaned me one."

Ryan looked up to see that Crystal had gotten to her feet and was now standing between her and Justin's bulky body.

"Well, Janna said she was asking you questions, practically forcing you to laugh and talk like old college buddies."

Ryan saw Janna flanking Justin as if she were his bodyguard. She had a smug look on her face that Ryan wished she could slap off. The face of a lying, evil witch.

"So what?"

"Huh?" Justin seemed just as shocked as Ryan was.

"Ryan and I were talking. We talk every morning. In fact, I think she knows more about me than you do." Crystal poked his broad chest for emphasis.

"You know her name?" Janna seemed flabbergasted at the revelation.

"Yes, Janna," Crystal announced, clearly annoyed by the idiotic question. "Not everyone likes being called by the name you pick for them. I know this will come as a shock, but some people actually like to be called by their birth name instead of *geek, fag,* or whatever else your small vocabulary can come up with."

Janna gasped in shock and Justin looked speechless.

"She's my best friend, so leave her alone!" Crystal demanded of the crowd that had formed around them.

"What about Justin? Your reputation?" Janna squeaked.

Ryan wondered how someone could be so worried about something so trivial and clichéd. Then again, as a total outsider, she really didn't know what kind of "pressure" students faced trying to maintain the status quo.

"I know it's hard to believe right now, Janna, but reputation isn't everything, and my relationship with Justin is as fake as those things you call boobs."

Ryan's mouth flew open at Crystal's words. Crystal was throwing away everything every teenager works so hard for—popularity. Crystal was easily the prettiest girl in school, and she had an attitude no one ever messed with and a heart that was filled with joy and care, although her other popular friends never paid any attention to it.

Ryan observed as everybody stared at Crystal in astonishment. When one tried to utter a question, Crystal shut them up. "I'm done with all of this crap. I'm done with popularity, this school and its stupid 'status quo,' and I'm especially done with you, Justin."

"You little bitch." Justin pushed Crystal up against the wall. "Are you breaking up with me?" With his wide shoulders and muscular arms, he had no trouble holding the 120-pound girl against the wall.

Ryan and Crystal began a joint effort to push Justin away. Crystal spat in his face and Ryan attempted to pull him back using all the strength at her disposal. She felt every muscle bunch under her T-shirt and her thighs strained against her jeans until both she and Justin and fell to the tangerine carpet.

"Is there a problem back here?" Ms. Adams, their teacher, had finally looked up from her computer long enough to see the chaos breaking out in the back of the classroom.

"No ma'am," one of Justin's basketball buddies answered for all of them as the big group that had formed anticipating a fight dispersed.

Ms. Adams watched as the kids took their seats and then turned to begin the day's lesson.

"You are dead meat after class," Justin whispered between Ryan and Crystal. Ryan didn't have to ask to know he was talking to her.

❖

"Baby, are you okay?"

Ryan snapped out of her thoughts and found ocean blue eyes staring back at her in concern. "Huh?" Dumbfounded after remembering her last day of high school, she couldn't find words to speak to her lover, Maxine.

"Where did you just go?" Maxine reached over the table to grasp Ryan's hand. They had been happily in love for the past three years, so Ryan knew that Maxine would not let this go with a simple "I'm okay."

Ryan looked at Maxine and finally felt at ease. "I'm so sorry, sweetheart." Ryan wanted to reach over and brush the loose black curl behind Maxine's ear, but instead kept her hand in her lap.

They might be forever lovers, but neither enjoyed a lot of public displays of affection, and Ryan was careful not to show almost any in this particular area. While she was eager to celebrate her father's sixtieth birthday, unfortunately that also meant visiting the place her parents had raised her. Bad dreams and random memories had been plaguing her since their arrival.

"I was thinking about a past memory." Ryan tried playing it cool so she wouldn't worry Maxine too much.

"Please talk to me," Maxine begged.

Ryan forced a smile to try to lessen the pain she saw in her lover's eyes. She nodded toward the back of the restaurant, and Maxine swiftly turned to look. "That woman is Janna Davis. She helped get me kicked out of school."

Ryan had told her parts of the story, so she knew Maxine wouldn't need much of an explanation.

"Is it hard seeing her?" Maxine gently asked.

"A little," Ryan answered. "It was just a bit of a shock. She came out of the kitchen with that stupid smirk." *The same smirk—blood-red lips curved in a pasted-on smile, and above, the eyes of a snake.*

"It looks like she went real far," Maxine said dryly. "A manager at a franchise restaurant in her home town. Sounds real exciting."

"Probably still as much of a bitch, though." Ryan relaxed a little, but tensed again almost immediately as Janna approached. "Looks like we're about to find out."

"I'm sorry, but do I know you?" Janna asked innocently. Janna had deep red manicured fingernails that could probably scratch a hole in diamonds, they were so sharp. Her cheap lipstick matched, but her makeup did little to cover the malevolent wrinkles.

"You probably know of her," Maxine jumped in before

Ryan had the chance to answer. "She's a well-known movie director." She proceeded to inform Janna of Ryan's latest success.

"Maxine," Ryan grunted. She hated for the attention to be put on her, especially in an area that hated her as much as she hated it.

"Sorry, baby, I'm just so proud of you."

Ryan laughed at Maxine's noticeable delight. She was clearly telling Janna that she had made a mistake all those years ago. Maxine laced their fingers together as the conversation continued. Ryan even felt her promise ring being turned and twisted up and down her ring finger.

"Actually," Ryan glanced at Maxine for strength, "I believe we went to high school together. My name is Ryan Campbell." At Janna's evident look of confusion, Ryan continued, "You probably would remember me as 'the fag.' I was the only out lesbian in school."

"Oh right." Janna gave an awkward giggle and stepped back. "Kids, huh?" Ryan could tell that Janna remembered the last day they had seen each other. For all she knew, everybody still joked about a day that had filled her with misery for years. Janna wasn't going to own up to her mistakes—that much was clear.

"I must be going now. Work, work, work." Janna giggled, crimson lips curved into the parody of a grin, and ran off.

"Seriously?" Maxine looked baffled. Her mouth, usually greeting strangers with a big smile, was now a straight line. "I guess you're right—she is still a bitch."

Ryan laughed halfheartedly at Maxine's statement. Then Maxine asked a question they both needed the answer to. "Why didn't you tell her how much she messed up? How you are this awesome director and people actually ask for your autograph? Why didn't you make her regret that day as much as you hate it?"

"Because the last time I tried," Ryan now had tears in her eyes, "it nearly killed me."

❖

"Justin, please." Ryan listened as Crystal yelled from behind her. "Just leave us alone. We won't bother you ever again." Crystal was in tears, sobbing out her words.

I'm so sorry, Crystal. You don't deserve this, I messed up everything for you. Ryan continued to apologize in silence. She knew begging for mercy wouldn't help. She tried to jerk around when she heard Crystal scream in pain, but Justin had too good a grip on her. He'd had that grip since she took her first step outside of her English classroom.

"Let me go!" Crystal yelled again.

Ryan attempted to squirm free, but it was still no use.

"You're going to watch everything!" Ryan heard one of Justin's buddies say.

"Please, Justin!" Crystal wasn't going to give up. Crystal was a fighter; she wouldn't let some idiots hurt them without fighting back. Unfortunately, Ryan knew from years of experience that only made it worse. "We are two harmless human beings, you don't have to do this!"

"I'm going to make examples out of you two! No one crosses me!" Ryan heard a whole group cheer that seemed louder than any film premiere as Justin pushed her into the boys' bathroom. He kicked a stall door open and gave Ryan her first taste of toilet water. Luckily, that's all it was.

I'm so sorry, Crystal, please forgive me.

He pulled her out, and as she took a big breath, he pushed her in again.

"Justin!"

Ryan coughed when she felt air against her face.

"Having fun yet, lesbo?" Janna whispered in her ear. She felt Janna's manicured nails scratch her scalp and twist in her hair. Justin let go of her neck and Janna used all her force to push her back down.

Ryan still heard the smack against Crystal's skin even though she was underwater. She fought with everything she had against Janna; she had been no match for football player Justin, but anorexic Janna would be easy. She slammed Janna against the stall's wall, and Janna shrieked in pain as she stumbled out. Ryan had just enough time to see Justin land another blow on Crystal before two jocks forced her into another one.

"Hold her down longer this time, fellas," Janna said from behind them.

And they did—they held her head down until her lungs felt like they were on fire, her body felt overexhausted, and her eyes closed in a peaceful sleep.

❖

"The next thing I remember is coughing up water and Crystal saying, 'It's going to be okay, stay with me, Ryan, please stay with me.' She yelled for help as I rolled over on the floor and puked," Ryan told Maxine as she drove to the drugstore. "She had done CPR with a few broken fingers, I was told later."

Now that she was finally confessing all the details of that terrible day, Ryan couldn't stop talking. It was the first time she had ever told the story out loud. She had dreamt of the day, woken up screaming Crystal's name multiple times, and reimagined it multiple times as she worked. "I felt so ashamed."

Maxine rested her hand on Ryan's leg. "Baby, the way you talk about Crystal, I'm sure she wished it was her instead."

"Why would you say that?"

"Because that's how I would have felt, and although I never thought anybody could love you as much as I do, I think Crystal did."

Ryan fell silent as she parked the car next to the local pharmacy. She called her mother to make sure her parents didn't need anything else. After that, they quickly grabbed Maxine's prescription, a few sodas, and some salty snacks for the movie marathon her dad had planned. Ryan glanced at the tabloids and chuckled as she waited in line. Knowing the real stories made these things much more fun. But when the woman in front of them murmured something about not having a pen, she couldn't help herself from looking up. The woman was completely submerged in her bulky purse, and the first thing Ryan noticed was a birthmark on her neck that looked like a dove.

"I'm sorry, I could have sworn I had a pen in here somewhere." Crystal's hands were still engulfed by the luggage. The clerk behind the counter, a pimple-faced teenaged boy with longer hair than Maxine's, looked quite aggravated.

Ryan was momentarily speechless. She loved Maxine more than the world, but Crystal was the first person who had been there when Ryan thought she was completely alone. There would be no one that made her forget that.

"Another Crystal Crisis?" Ryan laid a pen on the counter and watched every muscle in Crystal's angelic body grow solid.

"I'm sorry, did you just say—" Maxine appeared even more stunned than Crystal.

"Ryan?" Crystal said.

"It's me."

Crystal was speechless until the clerk coughed intentionally. "Hold that thought," she said as she bent to sign the check.

"Baby, I can get this, why don't you guys go outside and chat?" Maxine suggested as she looked between them. "I'll be right there in a few."

As soon as they stepped out onto the sidewalk, the reunion started. "I really can't believe it's you. How have you been? Wait!" Crystal held up one hand. "I know the answer to that, Ryan Campbell, the famous movie director that every guy and gal in the industry begs for a chance to work with."

"You've been keeping tabs on me?" Ryan felt giddy at the thought.

"It's kind of hard not to. I absolutely love all your movies. I would ask for your autograph but I don't want to bother you with stupid fan stuff."

"You could never bother me, Crystal," Ryan said. "But please tell me, what have you been up to?"

"I'm a school psychologist," Crystal answered shyly. "I couldn't live with the thought of kids going through what we went through and not trying to help."

"Crystal, I am so sorry," Ryan said.

"For what?" Crystal stepped closer and grabbed Ryan's hand.

"For the way it ended, all those years ago. For being too traumatized to tell an already homophobic principal what actually happened."

❖

"I need you to tell me what happened yesterday." Principal Malloy stared down at Ryan as she and Crystal sat in Malloy's office.

Ryan looked at the floor, terrified. She gave no answer. Her lips wouldn't move, and even if they did, there would be no sound. It had only been a day since the incident, and she hadn't told her side of the story to anybody—not even her own parents.

"I told you what happened! Don't make her relive it too!" Crystal was furious. Ryan heard it in her voice, and her arms were shaking like a rattlesnake's tail.

"Ms. Rowland, be quiet!" Principal Malloy shouted. "You could have made up the whole thing, so I need to hear Ms. Campbell second your testimony."

"Made up? You have video of Justin and his friends shoving us into the bathroom. Then she was soaked and I looked more beaten than one of Muhammad Ali's competitors after a fight. That isn't enough proof?"

The principal didn't move an inch as he ignored Crystal's outburst. "Are you going to start talking or not?" Ryan continued to stay mute. "Miss Joseph, please send in their parents."

"Bastard," Crystal muttered.

Their parents sat next to them in the small office as Principal Malloy launched into a speech about how he could do nothing if Ryan didn't tell him who'd assaulted her.

"Your hands are tied? Crystal told you everything you needed to know!" Crystal's father almost jumped across the desk. "They held her nose and mouth underwater until she blacked out. Then those idiotic, brainless boys freaked and ran. My daughter—with a fractured rib and broken fingers—

had to do CPR! You're damn lucky that she's a lifeguard or you might have a dead student on your hands."

Ryan looked over at Crystal's badly bruised face and wept. She hadn't known the extent of Crystal's injuries until now. *How could they?*

"I'll be okay, I promise!" Crystal mouthed as the five adults barked at each other. "This wasn't your fault!"

"I love you," Ryan sobbed back. They were the only words she could manage to speak.

"I love you too." Crystal cried with her.

"What do you suggest we do?" Ryan's father spoke over the girls' declarations of their first love. "I am not letting my daughter continue going to this school with criminals!"

"They are not criminals," the principal said, defending the little delinquents.

"They committed a criminal act and are therefore criminals! Right?" He looked over to Crystal's father for help.

"He's right! Those students should be arrested! This shouldn't even be a school matter!"

"But it is." The principal glared. "They were under our care during those hours, and therefore this is a school matter. I do, however, have a solution for your girls if you are willing to listen." He paused as they huffed in anger. "They both have enough credits to graduate early if that's what you all decide."

In the end, it was what they both wanted. They definitely didn't want to go back, and they didn't want to have to start somewhere else in the middle of their senior year. Unfortunately, that was the last time they saw each other. Crystal's parents had her visit relatives in Europe just so she would have a chance to get away from the small town and maybe have the chance to start being who she really wanted to be. Ryan's parents had allowed her to begin an internship a semester early to start working on her dreams.

❖

"It might have changed something for you," Ryan finally answered.

Crystal kissed Ryan's knuckles and said, "I was heartbroken when we parted ways. I think about you every day, but I wouldn't have changed any part of my life from that day forward. I'm happy, Ryan, really happy. And you?"

"I definitely can't say I miss this place," Ryan answered.

"I suppose not, when you have a beautiful girl hanging on your arm," Crystal hinted.

Ryan felt herself blush, just as she'd done in high school. "Maxine is more than beautiful, she's…everything."

Crystal laughed at Ryan's shyness. She stood on her tiptoes so that she could kiss Ryan's flushed cheek. "Do you believe everything happens for a reason?"

"Yes." Ryan looked over Crystal's head and saw Maxine walking toward them.

"I do too, and here comes my reason," Crystal reached around Ryan and tugged a woman into Ryan's view. She was gorgeous, about the same height and build as Ryan. Her dark brown eyes spoke volumes as they stared into Crystal's. "Babe, meet Ryan Campbell. Ryan, meet Robbie."

Ryan and Robbie shook hands while Robbie's other hand snaked around Crystal's waist. Ryan smiled at the sweet gesture and hugged Maxine as she arrived.

"You must be Maxine, I'm—"

"Crystal. I've heard a lot about you."

"And I look forward to hearing more about you," Crystal responded.

Maxine looked up into Ryan's eyes, blushing.

"So this is the famous Ryan?" Robbie whispered to Crystal.

"This is the one and only Ryan Campbell," Crystal said.

Ryan only observed as Robbie brushed a tear from Crystal's cheek. Then the two exchanged a few whispered words, but she didn't need to hear them to understand the gist of the loving exchange. Robbie was making sure Crystal was okay. They smiled at each other before Robbie turned back to Maxine and Ryan.

"Would you all like to join us for some dessert?" Robbie asked in a thick British accent.

"We would love to," Maxine answered, faster than Ryan could comprehend the question.

As they walked down the street together, Maxine and Robbie began to chat about life in California. Ryan could scarcely believe that just a few minutes ago, she had been reliving the darkest times in her life, and now she was spending a pleasant afternoon on an impromptu double-date with Crystal and her wonderful partner.

"How did you and Robbie meet?" Ryan asked.

"Three years ago she was at the middle school I work for to speak about the dangers of the Internet," Crystal explained. "Long story short, we hit it off immediately and she asked me out. I knew that she was perfect because she took me to one of your movies on our first date."

"You're making that up." Ryan listened with disbelief in her eyes.

"Nope, I figured it was a good omen." Crystal smiled. "Like, enjoy the future but don't forget what the past taught you."

"It was a hell of a past," Ryan commented dryly.

"It's also going to be one hell of a future," Crystal answered.

And when Ryan looked past the heartbreak and pain, she saw the future Crystal was expecting. She was able to see the hope and love not only in Maxine's eyes but in Crystal's and Robbie's too. She understood now that there was no changing the past but only taking advantage of the future she was given. She kissed Maxine's knuckles as her lover excitedly exclaimed about their life in Los Angeles.

"That's it, you all are coming out to Cali this summer," Maxine demanded. "No excuses."

"Fine." Crystal faked dreading it.

"Only on one condition," Robbie added. "We get to go to the gay parade."

"I guess." Ryan pretended nonchalance.

As the group laughed and Maxine pulled out her planner to set a date, Ryan took a moment to appreciate how much had changed since the terror of their high school days. Then, Crystal had helped her feel less lonely. Today, Crystal had helped her finally forgive herself. For the first time, she felt at peace in her hometown.

A Tale of Modern Magic
Olivia Dziwak

My tale takes place on World AIDS Day in December of a year now gone by. This day of mourning and celebration of struggling for survival is the one I will always hold dear as a day of confusion, of intense joy mixed with sadness. As much as I wish a World AIDS Day wasn't necessary on our planet, without it the social mix and atmosphere that were the key ingredients to my magical night would not have happened. I was volunteering at an AIDS dinner event, good gay teenager that I am, held at a recycled manor owned by the city and used for such somber and significant occasions as this. A whole group of my fellow Gay-Straight Alliance members had arrived along with me, all of us making the short trek from school to the house in giddy excitement at the change of scenery from our usual classroom.

Despite Canada's reputation for slushy winters, this early December day was a crispy autumn one, the cold air invigorating to us as we faced the prospect of spending an entire evening catering to and entertaining strangers. Yet, at the back of my mind I remembered that these were strangers facing a weighty reality. Still, we were a giddy gaggle of gay teenagers, brought short with nervousness when confronted by the imposing front door of the ageing house. Could we, the teenagers, epically tardy and chronically irresponsible, possibly be earlier than the adult organizers? Suddenly shy, we stamped around the entrance, utterly thrown off by the lack of obvious leadership. The excitement of freedom brought about from being unattended by our otherwise occupied GSA supervisor was replaced by fervent wishes he were here, to tell us what to *do*. There was no doorbell, for God's sake! Our knocks went unanswered! Could we just walk in? We had no idea who actually owned the manor—maybe someone *lived* in there! Eventually I, the bravest (and most obnoxiously outgoing), nervously ascended the stone steps and opened the door.

An empty brick hallway greeted us, and our obvious obstacle the door overcome, we trooped inside quickly to escape the cold. Despite being a small group we made enough noise with our restarted chatter to attract an organizer running about the house, and we were soon all roped into carrying boxes and setting up chairs in rows of increasing complexity. People began to pour in as time passed—both guests and organizers. It was one of the first times I'd ever realized how much of a *community* we queers really are; of course I don't mean to imply that everyone at the AIDS day was queer, but we did constitute a heavy majority. So the evening, with many a hand helping out, began to take off. Food arrived and I was faced with the dilemma of the less-than-popular teenager: who to eat with? At school I mostly avoided the cafeteria (the tables of cliques are like labels for sexuality, and I dislike and avoid them both) and just ate with whoever showed up in front of the library, so this seating dilemma was a legitimate problem for me. I hadn't been going to the GSA long enough to form good friends there, so in my desperation my instinct was to choose the person in the GSA who I had known the longest (though by no stretch the best). She was a golden-haired, artsy-type girl who happened to have gone to my elementary school and then popped up in my high school GSA out of the blue, to my surprise and delight. I think it's always great to find out people from my past turned out to be queer. It makes me think that had I been brave enough to come out then, I wouldn't have been alone.

So, this girl. Her name was Jane, and that was all I could remember from our bygone days together, besides the fact that we were both Polish. This turned out to be enough, however, because we soon got into a discussion about similarities between cultural foods (we were eating Iranian cuisine) and the merits of the yellow mushy stuff above all other foods being served. Mealtime having been successfully survived, Jane and I were sent outside to hang a newly discovered poster for the event and to round up any stragglers and send them the right way.

There I was, alone with a pretty girl who I was getting along with famously. And I didn't feel the slightest bit nervous! Why? I honestly, sincerely did not think I stood a chance. The thought didn't even cross my mind. How could it? I was a zitty junior who talked too much and too loudly, and she was the prettiest girl in the GSA, who had only deigned to eat with me because there was no one better around.

But this is where the magic stirred. For one, we were outside without jackets or sweaters and the temperature had been dropping steadily since our arrival at the manor, so it was *cold*. We were already giddy; now in the cold we hit full-out-hysterical-laughter mode. We had to struggle with a huge piece of plastic-y canvas stuff, try to wrap it around another sign, and then hold it down with twine, some badly sticking tape, and malfunctioning scissors. All as fast as possible because of the chill. The entire production felt like slapstick comedy. But somehow this mind-numbing temperature made two girls who had only ever bonded over yellow mush open up to each other. She told me how bad it would be if her parents saw this sign we were trying so hard to put up, and I told her that with our skills at poster placement it would probably just blow away anyway. She laughed. We talked about Polish families, how conservative they can be, how much we tend to stick together in Canada and how weird it would be if our respective younger siblings dated each other. And just before we reentered the house Jane, hand poised on the doorknob, standing two steps above me and looking lovely in the fading light, turned to me and said:

"You know, you'd be the perfect girlfriend. If you were a guy, my parents would love you."

I was deaf to that second part, for the simple reason that I momentarily stopped breathing and lost the ability to do anything at all but laugh nervously. Wild, leaping joy flooded me followed immediately with boot-shaking fear: *Oh shit, were we* flirting *this whole time?! I didn't know that! Do I say something? Do I ask her out? Is she asking me to ask her out? WHAT DO I DO?* Luck was on the side of the gibbering idiot that night, because despite having turned almost as red as me at her own words, Jane had the courage to follow up with, "But seriously, we should hang out sometime."

Hang out. Say all you want about the degradation of romantic language—those words held greater promise for me that night than any other two in my entire life. Sure, it wasn't a proper asking-out, nor did it guarantee an actual *date.* Or romantic feeling from her side. Or anything at all, except an interest in the brief connection we had forged. But it meant she was willing to let me stare at her in awe for a bit more, so it was good enough in my books.

We headed back to our volunteer duties. As I returned to storing away chairs after dinner, I couldn't help but wander the manor halls in whatever configuration I could to try to catch glimpses of her. And grin at her. And feel confused and awkward, walk away, freak out for a bit, and repeat. My suspicion grew with every moment; *I think she really likes me.* But here was an irrefutable problem: She also barely knew me. It wasn't like we had ever really talked before! So this was probably just a brief flight of fancy, a pretty girl taking pity on me. The only person who could convince me otherwise was Jane herself, who at a lull in our duties pulled me aside to an abandoned hallway where we both slouched against a wall. The conversation came round to the school dance that had happened a few days previously. I had gone to the dance with a small group of friends and spent most of the night with one in particular. We had teased each other into pretending we were a couple, since neither of us wanted to show up at the dance dateless.

"Yeah, I saw you guys dancing together. I was kind of jealous. I thought about asking you…"

I couldn't believe my ears. "No way! I thought about dancing with you too, but I figured you'd just think I was some weird girl from the GSA you barely knew…"

She grinned sheepishly. "I kept counting down in my head, saying I'd go up to you on three. I told my friends too, to try to get them to dare me to do it."

"No way."

"Seriously. You've been in my diary for a while."

No way no way NO WAY. "Wow. Thank you." It was the

wrong thing to say. Silence fell, and we both stared awkwardly at the floor. "I think we should date," I finally blurted out.

Jane looked at me with slight amusement. "Yeah. That's what I meant by hanging out."

"Oh. Cool."

"Cool." Silence again, but it was a delicious, adorable awkward this time. We smiled at each other and blushed.

Then it was time to go upstairs. I was far too terrified to kiss her like I so desperately wanted to, but she took my hand, and the pleasant jolt I got from contact with her skin was bliss. None of our fellow volunteers noticed our new hand-holding status, but as we sat together through the song-and-poem part of the evening, we shared our secret joy through quick looks and smiles. I was conscious in that moment, as I am at the time of writing this story, that I was experiencing a once-in-a-lifetime moment of romantic perfection, so I made sure to take in my surroundings.

So here was my community. People both straight and queer, who had come together to celebrate survival and mourn loss. I saw couples who had once gone through the magical moment I was in the midst of, and my younger friends who had yet to experience it for the first time. I saw people crying as we sang together at the close of World AIDS Day, and people comforting each other, and some people with no one with them at all. It was overwhelming.

That was the true magic of that night: the fact that it was overwhelming, exciting, and confusing, and in the landscape of my memory so, so *big* that it defied any single triumphing emotion. Wonder? Joy? Incredulity that I had discovered something so unexpected? Gratitude that we lived somewhere and sometime that allowed it to happen? No single conclusion could possibly cover it all. I could only hope this was only the first of life's magical moments waiting in store for me.

This has been my tale, of dating and being queer, and of the real world, modern magic that people can create simply by being together.

INDULGE ME
ASHLEY BARTLETT

I don't remember our first meeting. Or any of the times we met, not until I really saw her. They have all fractured and bled and coalesced into very vivid thoughts that I can't pinpoint in time. I know that in those early meetings I only thought about one thing: This bitch was old. Thirty, thirty-five, forty, fifty, it didn't matter. Just old. And I pitied her for it. How sad that this woman is coming into my bar (it wasn't mine, but I thought it was) and sitting alone and chatting up the young, hot bartender. That was me, the young, hot bartender.

I didn't know then that young and hot were subjective and I didn't know that not everyone wanted young and hot. That those traits weren't everything, and that more often than not, they were nothing.

It took weeks for me to realize she was charming. I knew right away that she was funny. Old people can be funny. But charming? No, only twenty-year-olds could be charming.

It was months before I realized she was sexy.

I had noticed, in some far-off, detached way that she had physical features. She wasn't just a body leaning against my bar. Though the body wasn't bad. She worked out. To have a body like that at that age she had to. Her hair was short. Buzzed in back and long up top. A good haircut. She had dark blond hair, but as summer progressed the sun bleached it lighter. I'm not sure when I noticed there was some gray in there. But I remember disregarding that as a sign of age, thus unimportant. I think, weeks, maybe months, later the gray was what got me. One of those moments of disabling clarity. I was pouring her a beer. She had her head turned, talking to some other regular. The lights caught the line of silver rings in her ear. Her hair was getting a little long, curling into the rings. And I was like, damn, she's sexy. Just like that. She wasn't pretty or beautiful or anywhere in between. She just went from old hag to sexy. I'd laughed at myself. Sexy? I had to be drunk. The beer I was pouring overflowed onto my hand.

She asked what I was laughing at. I shrugged. Handed her the beer. She smiled at me.

Those smiles, I found later, were an indulgence. Unlike mine. I handed them out like pocket change. Something I'd never miss. And I thought I was doing the recipient a favor. As if my smiles were coveted currency. They weren't. But hers were. She gave them to me because I was a kid, the same way she let me open doors for her. One night, it was after closing, she stayed while I cleaned up. I thought she wanted my company. Because she was old, clearly lonely. I know now that I was drunk that night. Too drunk to walk home alone. When we left I held the door for her. And she let me. She knew I needed to hold that door. I wasn't butch. But I wasn't not either. That's why I needed to open doors. Just like my mama taught me. She thanked me, as if she were incapable of opening her own doors, or pouring her own booze, or walking down dark streets alone.

My attraction to her became sort of debilitating. I could function. Even when she was standing in front of me looking all sexy. That wasn't the problem. It was me. I didn't know what to do with it. It had been bad enough admitting it to myself—I couldn't very well admit it to another person. So I flirted with her. Shamelessly. Just like I flirted with everyone else who asked me for a drink. There were moments when I panicked, sure I had given myself away. I wondered if I had said that comment with the right amount of flippancy. If I had smiled at her just a little too long. If I'd defended her against some imagined enemy just a bit too strongly.

All my worrying was pointless. She'd known the whole damn time.

It was my self-indulgence that eventually got me. The obsession wasn't going away. Obsessions don't work like that, fading quietly into the past. So I was like, fuck it. I was horny, drunk, stupid, bold. Why not just hit that?

I looked straight into her eyes one night and asked her to come home with me. She laughed and I laughed and I poured her another drink. I went home alone. Same thing the next night. It became a joke. Other customers got in on it. And every time I felt like I was dying inside. Twenty-two is like that. Every denial hurts. And every time you laugh it off like a joke. 'Cause you'll never admit the pain. That would mean you cared. I didn't fuckin' care.

I'd almost resigned myself to the fact that it was going nowhere. Almost. So when she came in and offered me the ticket I almost didn't take it. Just the show she'd been working on. Well, not just working on. Directing. I fuckin' hated theater, but that was still impressive. I was going to politely thank her and ignore the ticket. I was going to give it to someone else. I was going to throw it away.

I went to the show.

Maybe someone else would have been into it. Had an epiphany about the woman. Like, damn, she did all this? But not me. I was kinda bored.

I didn't tell her that, though. Instead I waited at the back of the theater after it was over. Watched the actors and stagehands and everyone else leave. When she finally came out the door I played it cool. Gave half a smile and half a wave. Didn't want to commit too heavily to my excitement. She gave me a nod. I waited. Watched as she hugged a couple people, said good-bye. And then she came over to me.

I thanked her for the ticket. Told her the show was great. Not a lie, exactly, but not the truth either.

She called me on the fib. Then mocked me for my politeness.

I asked if she wanted to get something to eat. It was late. There was a burger joint. She knew the place. Everyone knew it. It was in the middle of the two blocks queers had claimed in the city. Hard to miss.

We walked. We ate. She suggested a late-night coffee shop. We talked. Joked. Nothing new. Neither of us mentioned going to my bar. Our bar.

And that was it. I went home alone.

She didn't come in for a drink for a long time after that. An eternity. Fuckin' millennia. Two whole days. And when she did come in she greeted everyone. Laughed and smiled. Teased me. The usual. But when it got late she hung around. Asked if I wanted to get another burger. Said it like it was only more of the usual—as if we had added late-night burgers to our repertoire.

I wasn't stupid. I said yes.

After that it was part of our repertoire. A maddening

addition. She was even sexy when she ate French fries. Sexy when she drank through a straw. Sexy when she tore into a burger.

Something was seriously wrong with me.

I remember walking home one night wondering what the hell had happened to me. Girls hit on me all the time. I averaged five numbers a week. Hell, there was a chunk of wall behind the bar dedicated to the creative way women asked me to call them. I was young and stupid and sexy and I fuckin' knew it. Did I call any of the pretty, willing girls? No. 'Cause I was hung up on a chick twice my age who thought mocking me was a sport. And I liked it.

I musta been going downhill. Fast.

Until one night. It was late, almost closing. She had waited till the bar was nearly empty. I don't know if that was for her pride or mine. All she did was look at me and say, "Tonight." I swallowed hard. Put down my beer. Followed her out.

She could have been talking about another meal. Or a movie. Why not add two hours to the torture? She could have been offering more tickets to her show. But I knew that wasn't what she was doing.

We didn't talk when we walked to my apartment. Even when we got inside we just stood there and stared. So I offered her a beer. That was what I usually did, after all. She said no. Then she tucked two fingers into the front of my jeans, pulled me close, and kissed me.

The woman could fucking kiss.

All slow and torturous. Like she had forever. But I didn't have forever. All I had was right then. Right fucking now. I walked her back and pressed her against the door. Kissed her hard and fast until she couldn't breathe. Chicks liked that. But not her. Oh, she let me kiss her, but she slowed me down. Kept her mouth closed so I had to work to get in. Had to kiss her light and soft the way she wanted me to.

When I went to take her shirt off she stopped me, shook her head. Said "bedroom" and left it at that. It wasn't a demand or a request. Somewhere between, 'cause she knew I would indulge her. I nodded and turned, her hand in mine. She followed me to my room.

I think that was the only time I surprised her. She thought I would go hard and fast and stop when the sun hit my open window. That wasn't what I did. It wasn't what I wanted. Maybe I knew then that I had to savor her. Maybe I just wanted to indulge myself.

I stripped her down, kissing, tasting her skin. The freckles on her shoulders. Her scarred knees. That dusting of peach fuzz low on her back. She tasted good, so I didn't see any reason to rush.

We fucked. All night. Into the morning. Dozed in the afternoon. Ignored meals and coffee and beer. The sun started to go down again and all I could think about was the tone of her skin in the evening light. I wondered briefly what the sun would look like in her hair. Realized I'd never really seen her in daylight. But then she wrapped her tongue around my nipple and I didn't give a fuck about the sun.

I woke up at two in the morning. I'd missed my shift at the bar. I was alone.

There was a frantic moment where I looked for a note in my destroyed bed. I even went to the kitchen and searched the piles of mail on my table. There was nothing. And honestly, I knew there would be nothing.

Time should have slowed down for me. But time is a bitch and she never does what you want. I was kinda heartbroken in that "saw it coming a mile away" sort of way. Foreshadowing didn't make it hurt any less. So instead of counting the hour-long minutes until I saw her again, I begged time to slow down. 'Cause I knew she would be uncharacteristically kind and I couldn't think of a worse fate. More than anything I wanted something to say. Something charming that would make her fall into obsession with me. Or something poignantly angry. Hell, I'd even go for the long shot of something mature. I couldn't think of anything.

Her apology, when it finally came, wasn't an apology at all. It was pissed off and sad and directed at someone that definitely wasn't me. She didn't bother suggesting that she had taken advantage of me. Which was good, 'cause I would have lost my shit. More than anything it seemed like she was pissed at herself for losing a buddy to grab late-night burgers with. So I told her I'd never wanted a damn burger or a beer or to watch a fuckin' play. I'd only wanted to flirt with an attractive woman.

That was hard for me to say. It was the first time I'd actually said it. She was attractive. In far too many ways. In far too complicated ways. No, I wasn't ready. She knew I wasn't ready. That was probably what killed it. My inability to speak the truth and mean it. And my vehement insistence that age didn't matter only displayed how much it did.

Maybe we could have been perfect for each other. Maybe perfection has a shelf life. Or maybe I thought my pretty face was more important than it was.

She didn't come into the bar after that.

IGNITE THE SKY
JULIE R. SANCHEZ

Day 47, late afternoon

California smiles like the sun. She throws her head back, her blond hair windblown all around her. Her laugh is loud and clear and brilliant even over the steady hum of the engine and the blaring beat of the radio. She's radiant, glowing, blinding, gorgeous, and I can't help but sneak sideways glances at her as she drives her cherry red convertible down the 99. I hope she doesn't notice.

"You're going to get us killed!" I yell, laughing just a little, because her laughter is infectious and I'm not really upset at all. The late afternoon is smoldering orange, beautiful, ablaze; nothing can possibly hurt.

"Am not!"

"Are too!"

She sticks her tongue out at me. Then she turns back to the road. She cranks up the radio and steps on the gas.

The highway runs by below us. We speed along in the fast lane, passing car after car, the wind howling in our ears. I have never felt so alive. "Now you're just doing it on purpose."

"What?" she hollers.

"Trying to get us killed!"

"Maybe I am!"

And then we're going faster, faster, faster and I never want it to stop. But it's dangerous and wrong and I shouldn't want to go so fast with a suicidal maniac—even if she's beautiful, even if she makes my heart and my stomach and my soul clench in ways I can't explain—so I say, "Callie, slow down." When she looks at me, I can see my reflection in her white-rimmed cat-eye sunglasses. My own short brown hair is disheveled, and my white scarf is flailing. I look pale, and through the image of my own aviators, I can see the fear in my eyes.

"Why?" she asks, and there's something off about her tone. She's deadly serious, staring at me instead of the road, demanding to know why she shouldn't drive us straight into oncoming traffic.

I can feel the road and the speed and the hammering in my heart. I'm scared because she's so captivatingly reckless.

"Wouldn't it be better to go like this? If we live our lives as an adventure, there's only one proper way to end them. Don't you feel it? We're young and free and beautiful and brilliant and so perfectly alive. We're burning bright and fast, like supermassive stars, you know? And we can go supernova, ignite the whole sky in a fiery explosion when we die. Or we can just grow old, wither, let our outer layers float away as we wait for death to take us."

"Callie," I plead, hoping it's enough. "Don't." I can't say anything else because I'm not sure I can find the words to argue with her. My voice is caught in my throat. I don't want to believe anything she's saying, no matter how true it feels, but we're driving so fast, and I feel so perfectly alive.

She smiles at me, her teeth straight and white behind her bright red lipstick. She leans over and kisses me, quick and square on the lips, before turning her attention back to the road.

Then we're going faster, faster, faster and I know we're never going to stop.

Day 1, midday

It starts when I drop the pack of gum I'm about to purchase at the local 7-Eleven. I squat down, cursing under my breath, and then I catch sight of her shoes—red, strappy, five inches high. My eyes go up (even when I tell them not to), and I take in her tan legs, which go up and up and—and I have to force myself to grab my gum and stand. She's wearing a blue and white polka-dot halter dress, and between that and the curls her hair is set in, she may as well be a 1940s pin-up girl. She's gorgeous, and I try not to stare, not at her neck, her waist, her cleavage—not at anything.

"Hi," she says, shifting her Slurpee from her right hand to her left and then extending her right for me to shake, "I'm California. California Fiona Hadley, technically, but I've never cared for technicalities, so everyone calls me Callie."

I shake her hand because I don't know what else to do. Dumbly, I reply, "Grace Aldrin."

She smiles. "Do you live around here?"

Something inside me seizes up because I'm half hoping that's a proposition. "A few blocks away."

"I've never seen you here before."

"It's a pretty big town."

"It isn't, really," her pretty face scrunches in consternation, "not when you pay attention, which I do."

"Well," I can't help but smile back, just a little, "you probably haven't seen me because I just moved here."

"Let me guess." She studies me with her too blue eyes. "You have an internship for the summer. You're pre-law at Yale."

"Yes," I stutter and blink, feeling a bit breathless. "How did you know all that?"

"I know everything." She shrugs, quirking an enigmatic smile that heightens her intoxicating aura of mystery. "And I read your sweatshirt."

I blush as I look down at my own navy Yale sweatshirt, which I'm wearing not-so-stylishly with khaki shorts. I feel silly. I don't know what to say.

"Are you originally from somewhere around here?"

"Yeah," I nod, clenching the pack of gum tightly in my fist, "my parents live about twenty miles north. You?"

Her smile fades. Something flashes in her eyes, and suddenly, she's guarded. "I live here. I've always lived here." Her eyes flicker past me, through me. "Probably always will."

"Oh." I look down at my sneakers. There isn't anything I can think to say.

"We should have an adventure," she announces abruptly, and that carefree enthusiasm reenters her tone.

"You don't know me," I say too quickly, because I want her too fervently. "I could be a serial killer." I pause. "Or boring."

She smiles yet again, broad enough to show her teeth. "I know you well enough to know that you're neither of those things, Grace Aldrin. I know something else, too." She takes a quick sip of her Slurpee. Her tongue is stained blue. "We're going to have an adventure."

Day 47, morning

"Grace." Rory, the friendly cardigan-clad receptionist of Giles and Burke, sticks his head into the filing room. "There's someone here to see you."

I frown because I'm at work, and no one should be popping up to visit me at work. "Who is it?"

He shrugs, looking thoughtful. "A girl. She looks upset."

I drop the file I'm holding because there's only one girl I talk to who doesn't work here. I follow Rory out to the front room, and sure enough, California's sitting in one of the chairs. She's slouched over a little, and her hair is less than perfect. As I get closer, I make out the faint tracks of mascara on her cheeks. She's been crying.

"Rory," I say softly, without turning back to look at him, "I need a minute."

"Of course." He nods, but I barely hear him because I'm already leading California out the door.

We sit on the cement steps leading up to the firm's office. I drape my arm around her shoulders, and she rests her head against my shoulder. We take a wordless minute to stare out at the cartoon city, where the colors are too bright—the blue of the sky, the gray of the buildings, the green of the trees, the black of the asphalt, and the yellow of the lane lines. The world is humming, buzzing, twittering, bursting alive with action, but it doesn't look or feel real. We're three stories above the ground; the action can't touch us. It isn't real.

The minute goes by, and then California speaks. "I'm leaving. This town. Forever. This afternoon."

Suddenly, everything is real. Too real. It hurts, and I

forget how to breathe. I stare at her profile, and I can see her determination. She's serious; this isn't a joke, and she isn't going to change her mind.

"It's too much," she goes on. "It's too much, and I don't deserve it, so I'm leaving, and I'm never coming back."

I stare at her, and I feel my heart breaking. "You're right," I say as soon as I find my voice, "you don't deserve it. You never did. You should leave."

She looks up at me. "Grace?"

I smile weakly. "Callie."

"Will you come with me?"

I kiss her fiercely in response, letting the touch of my lips say what I can't vocalize. I pull back after a moment as soon as I remember where I am. I stand up, pulling her up with me. I ask her to wait for me.

I step back inside. Instantly, I'm under Rory's hazel-eyed scrutiny.

"That's her, isn't it?" he asks. He knows everything about her (except the bruises, never the bruises) because I've told him.

"Yeah," I nod, biting my lip nervously.

"She needs you, doesn't she?"

This, I think to myself, is why I befriended Rory. His intuition and understanding and classy purple cardigans. "Cover for me?"

"Of course."

Day 13, midnight

I don't ask how she got my address. I don't know if she followed me or asked the cashier at 7-Eleven or stalked me on the Internet. I don't care. I don't care that it's midnight or that I'm wearing gym shorts and a T-shirt. I see her standing across the threshold of this tenement I call an apartment, and I can't help but smile. She's a ray of sunshine in the bleak corporate monotony that is rapidly becoming my life. I need her more than I need oxygen.

California tilts her head to one side, rests a hand on her hip, and drawls, "Ready for an adventure?"

I can't see her eyes through the cat-eye sunglasses, but I don't need to. I nod, and in an instant, we're running down the stairs and out of the building. The only car parked out front is the cherry red convertible. I look at her, asking the question silently.

"It was my dad's," she answers, a shade quieter than usual. Then she perks up and gets in the driver's seat. "Hop in."

I get into the passenger seat.

She turns the key, starts the engine, and then we're off. She taps the steering wheel as we stop at an intersection. "What kind of music do you like?"

"Pop," I say, relishing the feel of the night air, the glow of the red light, the sheer magic of being next to her, "but not the stuff they play on the radio. Stuff that has folksy or bluesy undertones and powerful lyrics. Missy Higgins or Brandi Carlile."

She nods. The light goes green, and we move forward. "I like everything, but especially songs that are loud and have a good beat, good energy. Usually ska, sometimes rock, but never the stuff they play on the radio. So let's compromise." She shoots me a smile before switching the radio on. She adjusts the tuner until some hip-hop song I've never heard comes on, and then she turns up the volume. "If neither of us likes it, it's the perfect compromise."

I can't help but laugh at her logic. I can't help but drum my fingers against the armrest. It's chilly, but I'm not shivering. I'm exhilarated. "Where are we going?" I ask as she merges onto the freeway.

"It's a surprise." She goes straight to the fast lane; she speeds up, up, up. "People drive fast for the wrong reasons." She grips the wheel a little tighter. "They do it because they can, because we've designed cars to go fast, so why the hell not?" She shakes her head.

"What are the right reasons?"

She smiles at me. "Speed reminds us that we're alive, that we could die at any moment, and that we shouldn't want it any other way."

Day 38, evening

I haven't said anything. Not when she picked me up at my apartment. Not as we drove to the diner. Not once we sat down and ordered. Not now. I'm staring steadily at my strawberry milkshake, but I can't drink it or eat my fries because I'm too caught up on what I can't ask her but know I should.

California doesn't seem the slightest bit concerned with the bluish-purple bruise blossoming around her right eye. She doesn't notice (or doesn't mention) my preoccupation either. She just dips her fries in her chocolate shake and pretends that nothing is wrong. Maybe she isn't even pretending. Maybe to her black eyes are as normal as flying pigs or talking dogs. Maybe she doesn't care. She's her normal self, smiling and bubbly, when she asks, "So, have you told anyone about us?"

I force my eyes away from my food, and I smile back at her, as I always do. "I don't have many friends here."

"That's not the same as none." She squints at me. "I haven't, but I don't mind that you've told someone. Who was it?"

I don't have the slightest idea how she finds me so transparent. "Rory, the receptionist at the firm."

"Tell me about him."

I shrug. Rory is just Rory. "He's in his twenties. He takes classes at the community college in art history. He wants to work at a gallery someday. He wears big, thick Harry Potter glasses, but I don't think he needs them. He owns at least fifty different cardigans. He's gay. He's one of the best friends I've ever had." I realize I'm smiling, and I don't know when I started.

She smiles back at me, but it isn't one of her normal smiles. It doesn't reach her eyes. They are cloudy, more gray than blue, bordering on wistful.

"Tell me about your best friend."

"I don't have one." When she blinks, her eyes clear up, and she seems perfectly unfazed. "Any siblings?"

"A brother. He's ten years older, though, so I may as well be an only child." I take a sip of my milkshake. It's good, even if I'm not really thirsty or hungry or anything but nauseous.

"I am. An only child, I mean." She's so carefree, careless, pure, even when the evidence of violence is fresh against her skin.

"Callie," I say softly, staring at her as intently as I know how, "tell me about your parents."

Again, her smile is weak and forced. This time, she's the one who stares at her food without touching. "Parent," she corrects. "I never had a father. Or I suppose I did, once, but he left. Probably before I was born, but maybe just when I was too young to remember." She shrugs. "I don't know. I never asked. He left the car. That's it. It's fine. I like the car. I'm glad he left. It's better. He wouldn't have deserved—no one deserves—well."

I wait because I know she takes this game seriously, and if I just wait long enough, she'll have no choice but to answer.

After a long moment, she starts talking. "I live with my mother—always have, always will. I don't look like her at all. She's tall. She has a crooked nose. Her ears are missing a crease. Her hair is kind of reddish and long and thin. She never smiles. She doesn't leave the house. She has OCD. She's paranoid. She—" She breaks eye contact, looks at her food, and there's a second, a single second, in which she stops pretending. "Her brain's just wired a little differently."

"Callie." I seize her hand from across the table. I hold it in mine. I press my thumb lightly against her wrist because I need to feel her pulse, to know that her heart is beating, to remember that she is alive. "Does your mother hit you?"

She cocks her head to one side and smiles at me wryly. "It isn't your turn."

Day 14, before dawn

"Here we are."

California's surprise consists of a neighborhood park. It's small, sandwiched between two cookie-cutter suburban houses. It's run-down and empty and probably more than a little forgotten. The foliage is lush, green, overgrown. The playground equipment is tarnished with rust, but it still sparkles in the moonlight.

"It's beautiful." I'm a little breathless.

She just smiles at me in that funny way of hers where I

can't tell quite what emotion she's trying to convey. Then the moment's over, and she looks away. "Let's ride the seesaw. Everyone always talks about swings, but they're so cliché. Swings are solitary, and no matter how high you fly, you can't forget you're alone. On a seesaw, you can't forget you're with someone. You go so much higher."

I run over to the seesaw with her. It's not the normal "plank of wood on a fulcrum" model. There are two small benches, with a larger plank between them. We each take one bench. The wood is hard, unforgiving, and everything creaks when anything moves, but I don't care. I don't care that I'm trespassing or that it's midnight or that I'm wearing my gym clothes or that I barely know her. I don't care that I'm dying or that the sun is dying or that the universe itself is dying because we're on a seesaw, going up and down and up and down and up and down, and the night is chill, and the moonlight catches in California's hair. I don't care.

"Let's play a game," she says suddenly. "One of us asks a question. The other one answers. The first person answers her own question. Then the second person asks a new question, and then we start over. I'll start. If you could go to any decade, when and where would you go, and why?"

I laugh because it shouldn't be a surprise that she doesn't ask simple questions. "The 1780s," I find myself saying without really thinking it over. "I'd love to have been a part of the Constitutional Convention."

"Of course." She smiles. "I'd go to the 1920s or the 1940s because people didn't take life for granted after the wars. Probably the '40s, though, because they had better clothes."

I laugh. "What's your favorite color?"

"White," she says instantly even though I would have guessed red from her car, her shoes, her lipstick. "It's pure."

"Mine's blue."

"What do you want to be when you grow up?"

I'm laughing as I answer, "A Constitutional lawyer." I pause. "Or maybe one of those guys who reads the Declaration of Independence on the Fourth of July."

She laughs too. "I want to be free." Her smile disappears. "But not happy, never happy."

"Why not happy?"

"Because happiness is an illusion, and I want to live something real, true, gritty but pure."

"I've always wanted to be happy." I look away, at the trees, the sky, the slide, at everything but her. "I've never thought I could be." *Until now*, I think but I don't say that.

"Boys or girls?"

My eyes snap back to her, and I can see that she's perfectly serious. I blush, but I know I can't lie to her. "Girls."

She smiles that smile and the butterflies in my stomach start to flutter away. "I like everyone." Then she frowns, delicately, thoughtful but not upset. "Well, I don't actually like everyone. I mean that I could like anyone. It depends on the person. The good of the heart, you know?"

I take a moment to absorb what she said. I relish the up and down, the wood against the spine, the wind, the moonlight in her hair. I'm the closest I've ever felt to not dead, and I think that it's enough. Life; California; this moment in June.

Day 24, night

"Hi," California says as she invites herself into my apartment. "I'm sorry I didn't call or anything. I know it's late." She looks absently at the green LCD display of my microwave, which reads 3:26. "Or I guess it's early. I guess it doesn't matter because I've told you that I hate technicalities, haven't I?" She smiles, lets out a small laugh. "I do. I really do. They're perversions of the truth. They hurt, and—some hurt's good, you know, but some isn't. People abuse technicalities. They shouldn't. But people do a lot of things they shouldn't. I'm sorry. It's late or early or something, and I've woken you up. I should stop rambling. I'm sorry. I should stop apologizing when I don't mean it."

"Callie," I say because I've just woken up and I'm not alert enough to think of anything but her name, her smile, the way she can just go on and on and on without stopping to think or breathe or regret. "Do you want some tea? Water? I don't have much else."

"No, I'm fine." She looks around, her eyes darting, rather like a hurt animal. Everything about her is just the slightest bit off. Her hair is out of place; her curls are disheveled. She's wearing slippers and an Oriental brocade robe that doesn't quite reach her knees. She isn't smiling. "Well, I guess I'm not fine. That's kind of the point." She stops again. She isn't looking at me. "You should go back to sleep, Grace."

"I don't want to." Gingerly, I reach out, rest my hand on her forearm.

She practically jumps at the contact. "I shouldn't be here. I should leave. It's just," when her eyes roll up to the ceiling, they're wet with tears she refuses to shed, "I had to get away. I needed oxygen. I wanted to see you."

"Callie," I say because there isn't anything else I trust myself to say. My heart's too loud. Everything inside me hurts, and I can't help but think that if this is love, I shouldn't want any part of it. But I do. Because she makes me feel free and not dead, and I'm beginning to understand that that's infinitely more important than happiness. What I feel for her is real, true, and gritty but pure; this is the dream. I pull her closer to me, and ever so slowly, I wrap my arms around her. I lean close, close my eyes, inhale. She smells like sun and grass and wind and sky and summer. Then her lips slide against mine. They're soft, and her lipstick tastes like cherries. I run my tongue along her lips, breathing, biting, tasting, until she parts them. She's warm, inside and out. Our breasts are pressed together between us, and I can feel the steady beat, beat, beat of her heart. She's so alive, and so am I.

A Round Trip
Warren Smith III

I hear the familiar sounds of the train. I hear the people sharing their stories of daily life, the chug, chug, chug of the wheels moving over the tracks. I just listen and stare out the window. The world outside seems to be on fast-forward. As I watch, the train begins to slow at the next train station. The station fills with lights and movement and I glimpse a sign that says, Follow Your Passion. *It's just one of those signs advertising some new hotspot in the city, but instantly I remember that one night that changed me. How he changed me. A night I will never forget.*

❖

The train's whistle blew, followed by the conductor's shout of "All aboard!"

With my ticket in hand I got on. I was making my routine trip to work, and I took a seat right next to the window like always. I pulled out my little spiral notepad and placed it on the pull-out table. I carry it everywhere. Being a writer, it feels a part of me. I write all kinds of things: dreams, to-do lists, stories that pop into my head, song lyrics I hear on the radio. That day I was focused on figuring out what I was going to have for dinner.

"Noodles, spaghetti sauce equals pasta," I listed to myself out loud.

I didn't even notice someone already sitting in front of me until I heard the sneeze.

"Sorry. I didn't mean to disturb you," the man said.

As I looked at him, I was stunned by his honey-colored eyes—so stunned I began to stare. A few seconds ticked by before I came back to my senses.

"Sorry. No, you didn't bother me," I said, clearing my throat to seem less embarrassed at being caught ogling.

I quickly put away my pencils and pad while gesturing to the seat he now occupied. "How long have you been there?"

"Just after 'sauce,'" he said with a sly grin on his face.

I immediately averted my gaze out the window. Then I noticed his reflection looking at me with a generous smile. As I turned back to him, the smile took on a tinge of curiosity, as though he was trying to fit together the puzzle that was the stranger before him.

"My name's Zack." He extended his right hand.

"Ethan." I took his hand in my own and received the firmest handshake I'd ever experienced.

As soon as I touched his hand my whole body grew warm, the heat starting at my fingers and radiating throughout my limbs. The handshake lasted longer than usual, but maybe that was just my wishful thinking. After we exchanged names we rode on in silence. Not awkward silence—the kind of silence that falls between two people who have known each other for so long that words are not even needed. Just stolen glances and smiles were enough. It's pretty unusual. I usually only experienced something like it with people I'd known for years.

The train began to slow as it pulled up to a station with a Wild West theme to it, from the wooden frame to the rusted benches right by the entrance. It even came with its own fake tumbleweeds scattered about. As I looked around, a sign on the side of the building caught my eye—like the neon signs of Las Vegas but less flashy. *Follow Your Passion.* If only it were that easy.

I noticed the shuffling, strapping, and zipping of Zack packing up. Our eyes met, and in his there was a shadow of almost sadness or disappointment. But it quickly faded.

"Well, this is my stop. I'll see you later."

His tone went up as if it were a question. I don't know if I even had an answer, but I nodded anyway. At that moment I realized I really wanted to see him again, this stranger I'd just met no more than half an hour ago. I watched him go. After he stepped onto the platform he turned back and looked up at me through the window with a smile on his face. I couldn't look away, and neither did he—not until the train started up again. He slowly grew smaller until it felt like he had never even existed.

The rest of the day went by in a blur, a series of automatic movements at work like a robot. My body was doing the work while my mind was off somewhere else, filled with thoughts about what Zack could be doing. *I bet he's doing laundry right now. No, maybe working construction—even better, a doctor filling out charts and checking them twice.* Soon each fantasy turned into something a little bit naughtier then the first. In one I pictured us just sitting on the beach holding hands, and him feeding me strawberries. That scene quickly turned into a heated make-out session on my couch. Soon the image of him began to invade my work. His name would just appear randomly in the sentences I wrote, forcing me to reread, highlight, and then delete. I eventually just decided that I was done for the day.

I practically ran to the station, hoping I would get lucky and catch him on my way home. I took the exact same seat as before. This time I kept everything packed, freeing up the space so it was open for him. I just sat waiting. Waiting and smiling, like I had some secret. But as the train made its routine starts and stops, my smile gradually faded. The sun began to set, and with it, my hopes. Maybe I would see him tomorrow. But even as I thought that, I knew I didn't believe it.

❖

The next day was my day off, but I needed to run some errands and managed to convince myself that I simply had to take the train. I sat on a bench to wait next to a scruffy-looking man. He was in an awfully cheery mood, even humming to himself. Abruptly he turned to me.

"Today's the day."

Before I could ask him what he meant, the train appeared and I lost him in the tide of people surging to get on. Meeting Zack yesterday had been a nice departure from my normal everyday routine, and I decided to try to keep that feeling alive by not sitting in my usual spot. Maybe it was time for something new—to see what else I'd been missing out on by doing the same things like clockwork. So I went to another compartment. This compartment was filled with people. With more passengers I felt better, more alive. I began to put my bag in the seat next to me so they would think it taken. But as I was picking it up off the floor, a shadow engulfed me.

"Is this seat free?"

I didn't even have to look up to tell it was him, and I quickly placed my bag back on the floor. Zack plopped down as if the seat had his name on it.

"You weren't in our usual spot, so I went looking," he said with his charming smile.

The mere thought that this demigod was looking for me on purpose gave my body chills. Unlike yesterday's silence, this ride was filled with conversation. We were thirsty for information about each other. He told me he was an only child and seemed impressed that I came from a family of five. He worked as a freelance artist and seemed happy when I told him I was a writer. He even swore that when he was young he survived on peanut butter and jelly sandwiches for a whole year. That I couldn't believe. Who likes peanut butter?

That's how it went for the duration of the ride—us playing trivia Ping-Pong with each other. After a while I felt like he knew me better than some of my closest friends. The train came up to his stop, but he wasn't in any hurry to leave.

"Do you trust me?" Zack whispered with a mischievous grin and a look of steely confidence.

The warnings I'd heard growing up about going somewhere with a stranger were no competition for my instincts. I nodded, and just like that he was guiding me off the train. Our linked hands made me clumsy, and I swear I bumped every person or thing while trying to make my way out. We finally made it. We breathed fresh, crisp morning air that carried a chilly sting. Our eyes squinted to adjust to the sun.

"You ready?"

I was. We started walking, and it didn't take long for the city to meet us. It was just a small city—stores and apartment buildings separated here and there by a cluster of skyscrapers and a ring of suburbs on the outer rim. Zack, with his sure, even strides, became my tour guide and playfully acted as if I'd never been to the city before. Keeping up the charade, I gasped, oohed, and aahed. It was nice to see the city through someone else's eyes. Even though I'd been many times before, with him everything seemed so new and foreign. He wanted to point out the great places to dine, shop, and enjoy. But first we had to find something that was supposed to be better than all of that.

"This is it." Zack bobbed and weaved through traffic like a quarterback dodging defenders.

We made it safe and sound to the next corner filled with small vendors, each with their own cart of foods. He stopped in front of a cute little cart with a blue and yellow beach umbrella attached to it. Its specialty was pretzels. Zack high-fived the stocky man who ran it, and without even exchanging as much as a word, the man handed over two huge almond pretzels. They tasted even better than the ones at Auntie Anne's at my local mall. We settled in on the curb nearby and I devoured mine in two seconds. I couldn't help myself. Almond pretzels were my one true weakness, just like his was peanut butter and jelly. I guess he was paying more attention to what I said on the train than I'd thought.

With more than half of his pretzel to go, I just waited. I watched the variety of people that came by, from businesspeople in their suits and ties to the common people in their sneakers and jeans. I couldn't believe the day I was having thus far, so strange yet exciting. I was actually surprised at myself. I'd always thought of myself as a "stick to the rules" kind of guy. I plan and plan. But with Zack, I felt free to try things I wouldn't normally do. He made me feel more confident in myself. I couldn't believe that being with someone I just met could be so easy.

Zack leaned in close so I could hear him and asked, "What are you thinking about?"

"This is crazy, right? Are you not feeling a little strange? Do you just normally pick up strangers and whisk them off for an adventure?"

He just looked at me and shrugged, and with that we were off—up from the curb and into the heart of it all. In the beginning it struck me as odd that he could be so nonchalant about this, but another part in me was refreshed by the fact that he didn't think too deeply into things. He lived in the moment.

We window-shopped until we reached this small boutique called Che's Place. It was a store filled with an eclectic mix of clothing, from vintage to couture. I really wasn't looking but something sort of found me. It was a classic black leather jacket. I'd never owned one but had always coveted it. Zack noticed me openly gawking as he pulled it off the rack. He spun me around, and like a professional thief with nimble hands, got it on me in one motion. He then spun me back around to face a mirror that was off to my right. He admired his handiwork, patting himself on the back. I looked at myself—really looked at myself—and I liked it. Not just how the jacket fit me like a glove, but everything. Me in my simple gray cotton V-neck tee and black jeans tucked into my boots. Zack in his tank, All-Star Converse, and worn-in jeans that displayed skin through rips up the front. I liked how he made me feel special. I hadn't felt that way in forever.

After paying, we moved on. The jacket didn't come off once he'd put it on me. After finding the jacket, the rest of our day passed in a blur. There were just so many stores, so little time. I wasn't really even looking to buy anything else—I already had enough. With my new jacket and Zack by my side

I felt like a whole new Ethan. Zack's Ethan. An Ethan who could do what he wanted and say what he liked. It just felt right.

Before I knew it, the sun was beginning to set. Zack guided me up a few blocks to an In-N-Out on the corner. You could already smell the trademark burgers and fries a few yards away from the building. My stomach was growling with excitement. Who would have thought that shopping would get me that hungry? Like a gentlemen, he propped open the door for me.

"For you, my prince," Zack said with a smile.

"Thank you, my kind sir." I laughed as I passed him through the threshold.

When we had our food in hand we sat by the windows so we could watch the sun set. The sunset in the city is different. The fire-lit sky becomes the backdrop for the many skyscrapers. It warmed our skin and set us aglow. I looked into his eyes. By the light of the setting sun, they seemed awash in a rainbow of colors.

We didn't really talk; we just enjoyed each other's company. In sync with each other, our constant chewing and breathing created a sort of playlist. In that moment, I realized I never wanted the day to end.

Zack was the first one to break the silence. "You ready for the finale?"

I didn't even hesitate. I just nodded. By this point, he had to know I'd follow him anywhere.

As we exited, night was already upon us. The city had changed. It was more alive—thrumming with a new, more laid-back energy than before. As we took our first steps, we become a part of it. Zack hailed a cab quickly.

The surprise turned out to be Exotic, a nightclub I had only heard about in whispers from friends jealous they weren't able to get in. Even from outside, we felt the throb of the bass. As we waited in line we became fast friends with a small group ahead of us. That was something else I liked about Zack. Wherever we went he fit in, blending seamlessly with whatever type the crowd was.

The club, with its strobe lights, glitz, and glam, seemed like another dimension—so unlike the one we'd left behind at the double doors. The atmosphere was surreal, allowing the best (or worst) of each dancer to rise to the surface. Immediately, our new friends hit the bar. They ordered drinks with names you might think were jokes: Blackout Beaches, Fuzzy Nipples, Bahama Mamas. Zack and I passed the outstretched cups and bottles from hand to hand in the pack. Once they got their liquid courage we migrated to the dance floor. The music connected to a primal level in all of us. We moved and swayed, thrust and tapped. Throughout it all I felt at ease, finally a part of some bigger picture or plan. As I came back from my thoughts, Zack was before me—so close I could feel his body heat mingle with mine. My eyes traveled up his long torso to his broad shoulders before stopping on his face. It was as if the world slowed when we locked eyes. The music became stretched and warped like taffy. He moved even closer until we were chest to chest, and then he wrapped his arms around me. My arms instantly twined around his neck. He leaned his head down, slow and steady. My mind raced. Was he going to kiss me? Why was I nervous? Was my breath fresh?

All those thoughts ceased to exist as our lips touched. After a few sweet pecks he turned up the heat. His kisses become more forceful and passionate, and he even nipped at my bottom lip. What seemed like forever passed before he eventually pulled away. I slowly grazed my fingers across my lips in disbelief. The kiss was better than my fantasies. It left butterflies in my stomach and a longing for more.

He checked his watch and gave me the sign that it was time to leave. We said our good-byes to our new friends and headed for the door. I knew I'd never forget how the strobe lights revealed little glittered particles in the air. Even now, if I concentrate, I can still remember the smell of sweat and perfume that was the club itself, and how the music became a whisper as my mind focused elsewhere. Since the kiss, Zack hadn't let go of my hand. Fingers intertwined, we made it outside. The cold air slapped us hello.

We climbed into another taxi and began to backtrack. From the window I could see the places we'd visited that day. The now-dark In-N-Out sign, the now-deserted Che's Place. We ended up right where the pretzel stand had stood, marking the beginning of our adventure. Still hand in hand, we walked the rest of the way, both smiling uncontrollably like love-struck teens as we occasionally pushed and shoved each other playfully.

The city slowly started to dissolve and the train station finally became visible. The sun began to wake from its slumber. We waited on a bench for the train, wrapped around each other to stay that much warmer. We boarded the train, our usual seats now. As I began to come down from the high of the adventure, my head bobbed this way and that, trying to fight the good fight against sleep. Finally, it lost. Before my eyes shut, I saw the now-familiar sign: *Follow Your Passion*. It seemed that mine had found me. I didn't know where this journey would take me, but I hoped it would never end.

I hope it's a round trip.

Butch Fatale
Kirsty Logan

Tuesday night at the Sleazy Queen, three beers down, and Bex and I are sucking on a fourth and laughing at the hot femmey bitches: They've got the high heels, wet lips, shaved legs, soft tanned glitter-speckled skin; and Bex and I laugh louder so they'll look over. I hope they will, so that they notice the band badges on my jacket, so carefully selected to be the perfect mix of punk trendy queercore indie, including a band I don't really like but I know femmes like them and that's a good conversation starter.

Bex has her hair waxed, her quiff leaning off to the left, and *Beware of Clit Rings* she's writing on the bar. I know she's only writing that because her high-school ex had one and she's hoping the ex is here, hoping she'll see the graffiti, but mostly hoping that the ex will see her with a femme on each arm, and the thought will be in her head that Bex will fuck them both later, two dildoes on two thigh harnesses and four tits in her face and screams of joy shaking the windows in their frames and oh Christ I need to get laid.

"Bex," I say. "We need to get out of here."

"Mmm," says Bex, still scratching at the bar. I want to tell her to stop because any minute now the stoned-eyed barman is going to notice and kick us out, and that would suck because this is where the best-looking femmes hang out.

"We're just fucking around here. These girls will never go home with us."

Bex looks up from her artwork. "I don't want them to come home with me. Just to the ladies' loos."

"Jesus, Bex. That's so fucking depressing."

"You wouldn't say that if you were in a cubicle with your hand up her skirt." She nods at one of the femmes—dark hair, red lips, like the Bettie Page of dykes—and I have to concur. Maybe the goal for tonight *should* be the ladies' loos.

"Or," I say, not sure why I'm still flogging this dead horse, "we could go home, drink some beers, put on *The Crash Pad*, and fall asleep to the sweet sounds of lady-loving."

"Or," Bex goes back to her graffiti, "we could get some of our own lady-loving. Now shut up and drink up, or laugh uncontrollably so those girls come over to see what's so funny."

I go for the former, and down my beer.

❖

Three hours later the bar closes, and I leave. Alone. Except I'm not alone, because Bex is alone too.

"Well, that could have been worse." Bex leans on the rain-darkened wall outside the bar. I watch the couples all leaving, hand in hand or leaning heavily on one another's shoulders. High heels click on the pavement.

Bex pulls on a beanie hat to keep the spittle of rain off her quiff. She's wearing a plaid shirt over a black T-shirt, skinny jeans, and Converse with holes gaping at the heels. Although I haven't looked, I know she is wearing boys' boxers and no bra. She looks like a teenage boy. Then she speaks and you realize she's a teenage girl. Then you get up close and see the crisscross of lines at the corners of her eyes and mouth, the tension in her jaw, and she's only twenty-one but sometimes she looks a hundred years old.

"Crash Pad?" I say, leaning on the wall next to Bex. My head is throbbing with the click of the high heels. I can't stop thinking about how it would have felt to lick the pin-up girl's neck, the way her throat would arch when I slid my hands inside her bra, whether her skin would be sweet or salty. She clicked away twenty minutes ago with some other femme in a glittery dress. I try not to think about how ridiculous I would look in a glittery dress.

The traffic is crawling by and I know there's no chance of a taxi at closing time, not that we could afford one anyway, and it's not like our shoes are hurting our feet or we're cold in our plaid and denim, or like we have to get home fast because we've got to wash our strap-ons and find the right flavor of lube. I bet her skin would have tasted of chemicals from her perfume. She would probably have wanted to cuddle after she came.

Bex pushes herself off the wall and slumps off through the drizzle toward home. It's three a.m. and the bars are all closed and that ex never showed up after all and my clit feels swollen to the size of a ball bearing and no one noticed my band badges and I don't like the way that lipstick feels against my mouth anyway. So I follow her.

❖

Thursday night at the Sleazy Queen, three beers down, and I'm peeing and trying to figure out the graffiti on the inside of the stall door: names and lovehearts and song lyrics and scraps of poetry and across it all is *Beware of Clit Rings* because of course Bex has been here before.

I finish peeing, wash my hands, and stare at my face in the cracked mirror. I'm sure the shadows under my eyes are getting darker the more I sleep.

Back out in the bar, Bex is hunched over a table with a compass in her hand, scratching something into the wood. She's got her arm curled round so I can't see what she's writing, but if it's about damn clit rings I swear I'm going to dump my drink on her head. I sit down and try to see what she's carving.

"Where the hell did you get a compass?" I haven't seen one since I was at school. It's not often in my life that I have to draw a perfect circle, and thinking of circles makes me think of other round things like planets and globes and then of course I'm thinking about tits and it's not even funny how much I need to get laid. Next time Bex goes to the bar, I'm getting tequila.

"Brought it," Bex says.

"Thought you might need to draw some angles, did you?" I ask, but before she has a chance to reply I stand back up again and go to the bar because I can't even be bothered to argue right now about how fucking bizarre it is to bring a compass on a night out. The crosshatched lines at the corners of Bex's eyes look deeper than they did last week. I can't remember what she looks like when she's not squinting.

"Dos tequilas, por favor," I say to the guy behind the bar. He doesn't laugh, which doesn't surprise me. If I were him, I wouldn't have either.

I look back at Bex over my shoulder; I thought she'd still

be engrossed in her minor vandalism but the compass is lying limp in her hand and she's staring at the doorway. It's either going to be something really fucking good or something really fucking bad, so I take my time in looking where she's looking. The femmes are back, and they look so good it's got to be bad. The Bettie Page of dykes has a little peacock feather in her hair, and this seems like the perfect conversation starter because why else would you wear a peacock feather except because you want people to mention it? Every possible joke about birds trips through my mind before I abandon them all for being irrevocably shit.

I down both the tequilas and then grip the bar with both hands to keep them from rising back up my throat. "Same again," I choke at the bar guy, and pull a tenner out of my back pocket. I glance at Bex again and she's back to scratching, but with her back held oddly stiff like she's only too aware of the femmes watching. The femmes aren't actually watching, obviously, because why would they watch some butch in a plaid shirt and a wonky Mohawk carving a table? They have way more interesting stuff to think about, like how hot they look in their underwear.

I leave my change as a tip to the bar guy to make up for acting like an alcoholic, and take the new tequila shots over to Bex. We clink glasses, mutter *slangevar* as a toast, and tip our heads back. I wait a second longer to drink so that I can see what Bex has been carving into the table, which is absolutely nothing. Or rather, it's a fist-sized circle ringed over and over and over again, which is just as pointless as nothing. She slams down her glass and I look away like I haven't noticed, but when I look away I'm looking at something else and that's the close-up face of the Bettie Page of dykes.

"Hi," she says.

"Yeah," I say, and to my dismay I sound like Keanu Reeves. I try not to flinch.

"Can you settle a bet?" She perches one side of her arse on my chair, and I shift up to give her room. Then I shift back a bit so her thigh is pressed hard against mine.

"Sure I can."

She presses her red-painted lips together and pouts them out at me. "Great. Well, we—my friends and I—we were just wondering whether you're more a boxers or briefs kind of girl."

I frown, like I'm considering the question. "That would be telling." Unfortunately I still seem to be channeling Keanu Reeves, but it's okay because this chick is feeding me all the right lines.

"Well, I really think I should check for myself." She strokes her fingertips very slowly along the knee of my jeans. "Just to be sure."

I think about taking her on an immediate date to the ladies' loos and I think about asking for her phone number and then I don't do either, I just say "Want to get out of here?" and I know that sounds like a lazy line from a lazy rom-com but she seems to like it because she stands up and slips her hand into mine and smiles down at me.

I go to pick up the rest of my drink and I go to tuck my stool under the table and I realize I'm twitching my hand out aimlessly like a total tool so I abandon all that unnecessary shit and just squeeze her hand and walk toward the door and oh holy hell I'm walking out of here with a pin-up girl on my arm. Then—shit—I ask her to wait at the door and run back and say, "Bex, I'm just gonna…I just have to…" and she doesn't say anything, just grunts and keeps scratching away with her compass, so I just flick her quiff and head back to my girl.

❖

On our six-month anniversary, Amelle suggests that we go to the Sleazy Queen. We haven't been back since the night we met, and I remind her that there are reasons for our continued absence. Many reasons, in fact—most of them being bad music and cheap vodka and an eternally sticky carpet. But Amelle loves a bit of nostalgia, and if there's one thing the past six months has taught me it's that Amelle is extremely convincing. I'll have to draw the line at tequila, though; nostalgia can be really bad for your constitution. When we get there she heads for the bar and I try to get us a seat.

The Sleazy Queen looks exactly the same as the last time we were here. The lights are low enough that everyone looks more attractive and less drunk than they really are, the optics are snowed with dust, every low table is occupied by glittering femmes or wide-elbowed butches or a little bit of both, and in the corner there's a girl in a plaid shirt and hair waxed to a quiff. It's exactly the fucking same. The girl is rubbing something against the surface of the table and when I squint up my eyes I see it's a compass and then I feel dizzy and nauseous like I just huffed spray paint because it's Bex.

I leave Amelle waiting to get served at the bar and I walk over to Bex's table, standing there until she looks up. She doesn't smile.

"Bex. Hey. How's it going?" I lean down and hug her awkwardly, thumping my fist on her back.

"You know."

I laugh. "No, I don't know. That's why I'm asking."

She doesn't say anything else, just shrugs. She still hasn't met my eye. Amelle walks over with a drink in each hand.

"Hey," she says. She's got her hair tied back and she's wearing skinny jeans and there's nothing peacock-related on her head, so I figure maybe Bex doesn't recognize her.

"Bex, this is—"

"I know who it is."

Amelle raises her eyebrows but doesn't say anything.

"Can we join you?" I start to pull out a chair at her table.

"No thanks."

I laugh. "Seriously?"

"Seriously."

No one says anything. It's a standoff of epic proportions; I wait for a tumbleweed to blow past.

"Forget it," says Amelle. "Let's just go."

"Fine," I say, and I take our untouched drinks from her hands and put them on the table and walk out of the bar without looking back.

In the street Amelle walks on ahead, craning her neck to look for a taxi, and I stop to rifle through my pockets for a light. I get that sixth sense of someone standing nearby, so I turn around and there's Bex, scuffing her feet on the pavement and looking more than ever like a teenage boy.

"Um," she says.

"Bex, seriously. Did you take six months out of your smoker's lungs by running up those steps just to mumble at me?"

She keeps scuffing her feet on the pavement, and I'm getting annoyed at her and I'm just about to tell her good-bye when she says, really quietly, "I miss you." I don't know what to say so I don't say anything. "I should have called. I was just annoyed or…I don't even know. It's just…" She looks up at me, making proper eye contact for the first time. "Just fuck it," she says. She turns and starts walking back downstairs.

"Your quiff," I say, loud enough that she stops. "It's to the right." She doesn't turn around. "So does it change with the seasons, or what?"

She snorts out a laugh and turns round. "It shows the ladies the way to my bed."

"So listen," I say, and wait for her to climb back up the stairs. "You still got that *Crash Pad* DVD?"

"You know it."

I grin at her, and she grins back. Something wriggles in my belly, and I can't think of anything I'd rather do than go home with Bex and drink a few beers and watch strap-on porn. I look over to where Amelle is waiting for a taxi, but she's looking back at me. I run over.

"Hey, I have to—"

"I know." She smiles at me in that way she has, like she's got some fucking Guide to Being an Adult that I've sure as hell never seen. "I'll see you tomorrow."

"Love you."

"I know."

Bex is leaning on the wall, lighting a cigarette and pretending she can't hear us. She pushes herself off the wall and starts to walk down the street, her elbow cocked and ready for me to hook my wrist through. It's one a.m. and the bars are still pulsing and the rest of the night is spread out before me like a warm blanket.

And Bex is still Bex. So I follow her.

Pool of Sorrow
Sam Sommer

It was the summer of '62, the summer before I was to enter junior high school. This was something of a landmark for me, a turning point, if you will—a new beginning, like crossing over into another country. I knew if I let myself obsess over it I could easily fill my head with an eddy of swirling possibilities, the outcomes of which were at the same time both marvelous and dreadful. However, it was way too premature for that. School was still ten weeks away, and there were more pressing matters at hand.

My friends were all away that summer, off to camp or family vacations. It was the first year this had ever happened to me. In the past, there had always been someone left to pal around with—someone to share the swollen, sultry days of summer.

I was twelve that year, and the block where I lived was eerily quiet. By the end of July I'd read half a dozen books and seen three movies by myself (it was the first year I'd been allowed to do this). Then Teddy came home early from camp. Teddy lived just across the street. I was told one morning by a nosy neighbor who felt it her duty to keep the block abreast of all news, both public and private, that something had happened to him—that he'd gotten himself into some sort of trouble.

What that something was she never mentioned, or else didn't know. I didn't ask.

I watched Teddy every day for nearly two weeks from my front porch. At first he made believe he didn't see me, and I kept my nose in my book. I watched him mope about, watched and wondered how he could play stoop-ball for hours by himself, watched him pad around in his bare feet and swim trunks as he washed his mother's '51 DeSoto. The car had sat in his driveway unused since his father's death nearly two years earlier. His mother didn't drive, and Teddy had confided in me the day after his father's funeral that the car would be his as soon as he was old enough. I wondered at the time why he'd chosen to tell me that, or for that matter, why he'd bothered talking to me at all. Grief did strange things to you, I decided, and didn't give it very much thought after that.

Teddy was two years older than I. Two years seemed a generation back then. We went to different schools, had different friends, and although we lived just across the street from one another, it was only on occasion—usually when desperation prevailed—that we came together. Teddy was as handsome and as well turned out as I was awkward. He was almost a foot taller than me, a hand's width broader, and at least in my mind, a man. He had already begun to shave, although it was only a few inches of stubble around his chin and upper lip. He was at times brooding and inscrutable, and his silences were both devastating and exciting to me. I was terribly insecure and overwhelmingly attracted to him, and never at any given moment knew what to expect, but our mutual need that summer was greater than our differences, and it made us both more accepting of things we couldn't change.

After nearly two weeks of making believe the other didn't exist, we found ourselves face-to-face, quite by accident, by the oddest of matchmakers—the Good Humor Man. I hadn't seen Teddy on the opposite side of the truck (if I had, I most probably would have waited a while to purchase my ice cream), nor he me, until it was too late. By then it was impossible to ignore the other.

"Hi, Teddy. Getting a Good Humor?" I asked, too surprised to think of anything else to say.

"What does it look like?" he answered, sarcastically.

"Stupid question, huh?" I humbled myself.

He nodded, but then smiled. We paid for our ice creams, pocketed the change, and stood there staring at each other until the Good Humor Man got into his truck and drove away.

"You want to sit on my porch?" I asked, unwrapping my Toasted Almond Pop.

"Okay," he said, much to my amazement.

The rest came surprisingly easy. It seemed that was all we had needed—just a little push. At first, we sort of drifted together each morning. I'd wait for him on my front steps and wave when he came outside, or on occasion, he'd pace in front of my house, bouncing his Pensy Pinky off the curb, trying to appear nonchalant. Eventually, as the days progressed and we became more comfortable and accepting of each other's company and our new friendship, we let go of appearances. It no longer seemed important that I was the little twerp from across the street, or he, one of the "big kids." There was no one left on our block that summer to see us or care, and our mothers were both just glad we had found each other.

Teddy's mom seemed fragile and withdrawn to me. She hardly ever got dressed, and remained in curlers and a bathrobe most, if not all of the day. She'd sit at the kitchen table or on the back porch, read her paper, and drink cup after cup of black coffee. She'd smile benignly at me, or ask how my mother was when we passed each other, and then go back to reading. My mother had once mentioned that Teddy's mom had sort of given up after her husband had died, only she didn't seem sad to me, or heartbroken, just worn out, like an old T-shirt you could almost see through.

July had been hot, but August was brutal. It never seemed to cool down. Not even at night. We didn't have air-conditioning. It wasn't that we couldn't afford it, just that my parents insisted that it wasn't necessary. "The house has good cross-ventilation," they'd reiterate year after year. "I have better places to put my money," my father would say, and then quickly change the subject before I had the chance to object. The fact was they were both right. On most evenings it was cool enough. Only after two weeks of daytime highs in the nineties, and nights that rarely dropped much below eighty, cross-ventilation just didn't hack it. It was during that long heat spell that I found myself thinking a lot about Teddy and often dreamed of him.

The radio said it was already eighty-six degrees at nine that morning. I poured myself some cereal, ate while I dressed, and went out to look for Teddy. I found him by accident, sitting on the floor of his utility shed, crying. I hadn't meant to intrude or surprise him. The door to the shed was open and so I just walked in. When I saw him sitting there that way, I tried to back out quietly before he noticed me, but I wasn't fast enough. He wiped at his eyes and nose with the bottom of his shirt.

"I'm sorry," I said. "I didn't mean anything. I was just looking for you."

He stood up. "Don't go," he said. "I'm okay. It's nothing, really."

"How come you're in here?" I asked.

"The pool," he said, pointing to the large cardboard box in the corner.

I'd forgotten his family had a pool. It was one of those pre-fabricated things with the plastic liners, about three feet high and ten or twelve feet in diameter. I hadn't seen it in a couple of years—not since his father had died.

"My dad and I made a big thing of setting it up every year," he said, as if he had just read my mind. "I thought since it's been so hot I'd drag it out and put it together."

His face suddenly started to tense and I could tell he was going to start to cry again.

"I miss him so much," he said, holding back the tears. "I want him back. It isn't fair. It's just not fair!"

I didn't know what to say to him.

"Will you help me, A.J.?" he asked, and wiped at his face.

"Help you do what?"

"Set up the pool. We can use it for the rest of the summer."

"Can we?" I asked. "I mean, will your mom let you?"

"I already asked her. She said it was okay."

"Sure I'll help you, Teddy. It'll be great! Just you and me."

"Don't tell anybody that I was crying, will ya?"

"I won't tell, Teddy. I promise."

It took most of that day to set up the pool, and all evening to fill it, but our hard work was worth it. We had great fun, and I'd never felt closer to anyone than I did to Teddy that day. We had worked together like a team, and although I had the feeling that I was a poor stand-in for his father, I also had the feeling that Teddy really appreciated my presence. Without knowing it, I'd passed over into some new territory in Teddy's mind, and he began to talk to me about things I had the feeling he'd never spoken about with anyone else. My new standing made me feel special and scared me at the same time. I wasn't equipped to handle the width and breadth of what sometimes came pouring out of him, until it dawned on me that all Teddy really wanted and needed was someone to listen to him. I could do that, and I did.

Mostly what he talked about in the weeks that followed was his father. It seemed they had the kind of relationship that I knew I'd never have with my own father, that I'd seldom seen with any of my friends, and that I suspected didn't often exist. Like so many of the things that we need to remember in a certain way, they often take on a life of their own. So it may have been with Teddy's memories of his father—the idealized man he wished to hold on to and cherish. Or just maybe they did have something very special. It didn't really matter. What did matter was the loss and acute pain. It had been two years since his dad had died and Teddy was just beginning to deal with it. His words often left me feeling frustrated and confused. I tried to relate, but found it difficult. That sort of loss still wasn't in my vocabulary of experiences and emotions. My dad and I were hardly the best of friends, but I was suddenly very glad he was still alive.

I suspect I fell in love with Teddy that summer, or at least with the idea of being in love with him. What he felt for me I would never know.

The unrelenting heat continued on throughout August, and most days we spent swimming around in circles in the pool we'd put together, or playing badminton, or just hanging around up in Teddy's room. Sometimes I felt guilty that we were spending so much time at his house. My mom hardly ever saw me anymore, although she knew where I was, and that seemed to satisfy her. On a number of occasions I asked Teddy if he wanted to come over to my house, but he usually just shrugged, or simply said no, or else he ignored the question completely. He seemed more comfortable surrounded by what he knew, what was familiar, and I would notice that Teddy's mother (who didn't react to most things), did seem much more relaxed when Teddy was nearby. Besides, Teddy had the swimming pool—the deciding factor in the sweltering summer.

I knew the time would soon come when our friends would return from camp, or vacation, and with that, Teddy and I would most probably go back to the way things were before—before propinquity brought us together and changed everything. I hoped I was wrong, only I knew better. Perhaps that was why Teddy initiated the game that day, and why I so willingly allowed myself to go along with it.

Teddy seemed different that day: distracted, moody, somewhere else. He was quieter than usual and made a big deal over who wore which snorkel and which mask, and that we had to wait until his mother went up to her room to take her afternoon nap before we could go into the pool again. He said it was because we had just eaten, but I knew that wasn't why. It had never stopped us before.

"Watch this," he said, putting the snorkel in his mouth and clearing his mask. He took the old skeleton key we sometimes played with in the pool when we pretended to search for sunken treasure and threw it up into the air. It entered the water with a small splash. Teddy dove down to get it, coming up just in front of me. "Now it's your turn," he said, and handed me the key. I took it from him and repeated the process. When I came up, Teddy was behind me. He put his hands around my waist and told me to swim. "Let's see how long we can pull each other around the pool."

"Okay," I said, and put my face back into the water, continuing to breathe through the snorkel. Suddenly I felt Teddy's left hand move off my waist and down my stomach to my crotch. He just left it there, waiting to see what I'd do. I didn't do anything. I couldn't. Desperately, I concentrated as hard as I could on circling around the inside of the pool, but my body had a mind of its own and before very long Teddy had the answer he'd been waiting for. He reached inside my trunks and began to fondle my now fully erect penis. Breathing through the snorkel was suddenly significantly more difficult. Then, when it was my turn to hold on to Teddy, I reciprocated in kind, finding his penis already hard and a great deal bigger than I had expected. I had to wonder if I'd be so fortunate in a few more years.

I could have floated around the pool like that all day long, until both of us looked like prunes, but after maybe ten or fifteen minutes (I'd lost all track of time), Teddy suggested we go inside. He said he had something in his room he wanted to show me. We dried off quickly and quietly entered the house so as not to disturb his mother, then gingerly climbed the stairs to his room. I didn't know what to expect, and my heart felt like a jackhammer in my chest.

The room was heavy with expectation and smelled of chlorine from our suits. Teddy locked the door behind us.

"Take off your bathing suit so you don't drip on the rug," he directed me, while he stripped his off. I watched him as he did it. I took my suit off, feeling more embarrassed than I'd ever felt in my life, and rolled it up inside my towel.

Teddy pulled back the sheets on his bed and got in. "Come in with me," he said. "It feels nice." I got in next to him and stared up at the ceiling, afraid to look anywhere else. I was too nervous to move. All I could hear was the sound of my own blood rushing through my ears. Teddy tentatively placed his hand on my shoulder. I knew I had to look at him. When I did he just smiled at me and pulled me over to him. Our bodies smelled of summer, suntan lotion, and the pool. Teddy pulled me on top of him. He held me so tight that I thought I'd have to stop breathing. Then he rolled us over onto our sides. That was when he kissed me. It wasn't much of a kiss, but it was enough. We continued to hold on to each other, rubbing our bodies together until Teddy came. Teddy just lay quietly next to me, his face in his pillow. We said nothing for a long time.

"You won't tell anyone," he finally said, without looking at me.

"No," I answered. "Of course not."

I suddenly felt horrible. Not at what we had done, but because I had no one to talk to about what I was feeling, or about Teddy's tears that day in the shed, or all the things he'd talked to me about over the last few weeks, or the fact that I somehow knew Teddy and I would never be together like this again. At that moment I thought I'd explode.

Teddy rolled over to face the wall.

"I think what I miss the most is when my dad would come into my room at night, before I'd go to bed," he said quietly, and with more sadness than I ever imagined possible. "We'd talk about what I'd done all day, and what he'd done, and then he'd hold me tight in his arms for a few minutes and stroke my back until I fell asleep." He was silent again before he added. "It was a long time ago. I was very little."

I hesitated, unsure of what to do, but then placed my hand on Teddy's back and began to rub him ever so lightly. That's when I heard him say, *I love you*. But I was never sure if he was talking to his father, or to me.

MY LIPS
JOSEPH AVIV

When I'm two, my lips loosen in parted bliss as my mother tickles my back in slow rhythms. She coos in her native Hebrew tongue and traces her finger-rakes across my skin, stilling the rise and fall of my soft torso. I delight in being her greatest dependent, the younger child. Julie, a year my senior, is a brave pioneer, paving the way for me, and I am a lucky boy without reason to fear the future.

Our father is gone when we wake, and the yard is fresh for play. When it rains, we watch with an almost religious awe, and, indoors, create forests of sheets and sofa cushions. I play dress-up with Julie, and our mother stands by the kitchen window, not allowing us to know her, a young stranger kept so far from home. Swimming in silliness, Julie and I will not realize that we, like the rain, have kept her inside.

❖

When I'm three, my lips sing nonsensically into the space above our kitchen table. Perched on a high chair and with an occasional tug at the itchy elastic of a birthday hat, I faintly offer wishes to myself, *Abby ber day do you, abby ber day do you.* My mother has made a chocolate cake, and my father, always on the opposite side of the camera, documents the event. His father, a once-tyrannical dad and a retired dentist, is my eccentric, animated grandfather. He enters the room flailing his arms and shaking his hips, singing, "It's birthday time for *Josephy*, it's birthday time for the *guy*!" I watch him, fascinated in my high chair. A flustered toddler, I am hardly a "guy." A combination of clown and hermit, he makes a strange guy himself.

My father sits silently behind his video camera, zooming in. Grandma and Aunt Karen sit at the table, shielding their faces from my father's camera. "I didn't have time to put my face on today," one pleads. "Oh you *poor* thing, Scarlet," the other shoots back, placing her finger over a mole.

Later, Grandpa crawls on the floor, snapping his teeth like a crocodile, and Julie and I take turns on his back. There is a tinge of danger in the sharp, jerky movements and loud nasal voice that accompany his antics. Julie and I shriek with laughter when we sense the aggression rising in this large man body. It's all play, but the proximity between affection and danger is a new thrill, a possibility.

❖

When I'm four, my lips fold inward like kneaded dough. I realize for the first time the power of my words and the power of my silence. We've made the move to Israel, but I have not. My teachers do not acknowledge my words in English. It is their way of helping me to make the transition. Instead of asking for *mayim*, "water" in Hebrew, I remain thirsty. We take walks through broken gravel and orange orchards, through wood chips and plastic slides. Palm leafs and stray cats decorate the sandy ground plains of our new world, where I spend more time alone by the playground fence.

❖

In bed, I wait for my mother, needing the tickly curls of her mane, the smiling eyes, the animated voice. When it is my father who enters, I try to brush him off, to pick him out like eggshell from batter. He does not know how to express hurt. If he is broken, he is also invisible. He is a fuzzy, unthreatening monotone. And I, demanding his leave, am impatient and hot-tempered, my thick brown hair needing to be smoothed. I continue to wait for my mother. When my eyes have closed for the night, sending me to an ocean of warmth, my mother will read her Hebrew mystery novel in bed, and she too will wait.

❖

When I'm four and a half my lips stretch outward in a tightening circle, releasing shrieks of pain. Every morning, my nursery teachers try to calm me as my mother stands outside the door, waiting to hear the tears stop and holding back her own. We've returned to New York, to an apartment near the site of my father's childhood. In Israel, bombs are scattering certainty, and my grandparents are mourning the departure of their American grandchildren. Julie and I hurriedly enter picture frames on their nightstands. We smile simple smiles, me with thick eyelashes and gaps in my teeth, Julie under a curly black mop of hair, eyes blue and curious. It is inconsequential to me that I've visited a bomb shelter this year, that I've worn a gas mask. I am more shaken by the crying that pulses through me on school mornings. When it stops, I explore the toys of the classroom's perimeter, and I make crayon irises on paper, holding the crayons stiffly, but smoothing them across the page in a soft, raking rhythm.

❖

When I'm five, my lips pout and yank my brows downward in selfish frustration. My lifted arms are met with apologetic refusal for the first time. Walking on my own feet becomes what I deem a premature necessity. We are in Disney World, and a secret intruder has removed our mother from us. Our father becomes newly present, mediating between myself and my mother, who grows faint and removed. A new sparkle in her eyes startles me, and I can't reach it. She is distracted from my extended arms, and my father tries to hush me.

Julie leads me away into a fantasy of dancing puppets and lights that flicker in the dark. "It's a small world" echoes in the black cave water of the ride. Julie smiles sweetly. In my torment, her ease is an inaccessible enigma of innocence and maturity. She is an example for my own growth, everyone says.

When back at home, tears collect in the corners of my nauseated, pregnant mother's eyes. She lies imprisoned on our couch with pulled hair and other marks of her needy kindergartener. She is defenseless against my nagging and stunned by my inability to empathize. I have tugged on her, pleading for her to return into herself, to attend to me again, but I've failed and left her biting her lip to hold back the pain.

❖

When I'm six, Zoe's tiny head attracts my lips. It's like a warm ball of dough lined with soft peach fuzz. I can't seem to kiss her enough, and I share in my mother's delight. Julie and I sit on either side of my mother, soaking in the special voice and touch offered to the new baby. It's been a while since we've heard this sugary voice, but it never disappears after Zoe's birth. She will always insist on diminutive affection; she will fear growing up and fight it like a disease. When I am in college and return for visits home, she will cling to me, hiding in nurture and reassuring herself that the real world is still a world away.

Becoming an older sibling places me in an unfamiliar role, one that I ought to be very proud of, according to my relatives and friends of my parents. I grow fascinated with Zoe, my perfect little sister. We dress her in fuzzy winter hats decked with silk-rose garlands. In the winter I watch my mother transform her into an Eskimo bundle, a picture-perfect munchkin with lips that pout for a beloved pacifier. Zoe changes me. With her in my arms, I become aware of myself as a superior, a protector. I look to my mother and imitate her verbal gestures, squeaking to Zoe for a smile. The house is warm with a new tenderness that she's brought, and we feel more than ever like a family.

On Saturday afternoons, we play with Zoe while my mother prepares brunch and my father sits by the computer or reclines on the sofa. Sometimes when my father lies down to read his dental periodicals, we sit on him or tug at his glasses, pulling them off his face and sometimes putting them over our own eyes. His matter-of-fact annoyance both embarrasses and encourages us, and we continue to search for him, to remove invisible barriers between us, to try to see what he sees.

❖

When I'm nine, my lips strike me in my bathroom mirror as I brush my hair before bed. I think that they are red—lipstick red. We've eaten spicy tomato sauce at dinner. My lower lip is full, but hungry for stimulation. Ice cream, smacking, kisses. I tilt up my chin and watch my lips become seductive against my long, thick eyelashes. I am a nine-year-old boy feeling beautiful in secret. This feeling is foreign to Julie, I think, and I keep it from her. Julie has become a model big sister and a responsible, freckled treasure. My mother reserves special feelings for her, I think, which she releases in smiles and affectionate sounds offered at unpredictable moments. When she is pinning up Julie's hair for a ballet lesson or painting her nails against tissue sheets on the carpet, a part of me becomes raw, and I bandage it with spunk and feigned arrogance.

In the car, on one trip to Staples for school supplies, I tell my mother that I fear I could be gay. I've heard the word only a handful of times, and it's always felt foreign, irrelevant. But I've decided that normal boys don't want to be beautiful. My mother assures me that I am much too young to worry about such things. I'm not gay, just sensitive. I have two sisters, after all.

Rooted in my mother's nest and shielded by Julie's arms, I grow in a secret place, dancing wildly in my sanctuary and finding sleep still in the strokes of my mother's fingers. Zoe, now a preschooler, quietly observes my hyper antics. Sometimes she joins me, leaping through the house and using silly voices to tease Julie, who sits in a practical quiet and rolls her eyes, secretly jealous I hope.

❖

When I'm twelve my lips stiffen and resist themselves. Their inactivity spurs a new increase of motion in my brain. To my surprise, my body is growing into a guy. No longer a boy, I am faced with new rules of personal expression and social decision making. In a crowded cafeteria, guys sit in rows, the cute ones with spiky hair and athletic T-shirts. I've tried to put gel in my hair, but my brown waves will not yield to hard lines. I decide to train myself at home. The easiest way to be a guy, I find, is to be silent. Silence can imply strength. Julie teases me for the pseudo-spikes in my hair and the new Adidas wardrobe. She has found a comfortable circle of friends and dresses in simple sweaters. My mother must assume that I've begun my journey to manhood. I sense a distance between us, and I think she is trying to let go of me, to encourage my growth. I am falling inside, afraid and uncomfortable with where I am going. Stifled smiles and unspoken words accumulate and roll like marbles in my head, side to side in painful and distracting chaos. My lips, like locked doors, refuse to release them. They assume a new rigidity, a painful distance from the nights spent loosely parted against my pillow when my mother stroked my back.

❖

When I'm fifteen, my lips betray me—or rather, their paralysis betrays me. My numbness is a stubborn one, Novocain from the inside. My lips use silence to conceal—but sometimes silence is the most revealing. "Does it have something to do with sexual orientation?" my mother asks me at my bedside, noting the fragility in me.

Today I thank my lips for having kept shut—contort though they did against my salty pillow that night. I thank them for knowing that the impulse of an excusing "no" would surely have buried me. The next morning I trot silently down the hallway in my plaid pajama pants, hiding from my parents under lowered eyelids. I search for the feeling of relief that I'd hoped for. In the kitchen, in the bedroom, in the yard—it must be hidden somewhere.

I've asked my mother not to inform my father yet.

❖

When I'm seventeen my lips pucker for photo shoots alongside superficial girlfriends, who sometimes, in moments of empathy, hold my head still for me, calming the marbles that swirl within it. These girls restore in me a lost impulse for affection. The guys at school are awed, playfully begging for tips on getting girls.

My father picks me up from school, and on the way home I recline against the black leather, flipping stations to avoid the gloom of his silence, which is broken only by his deep sighing. On one such car ride, in an attempt to test his sensitivity, I'll answer truthfully to the scripted question, "How is school?" I will discuss the bonds I share with my female friends, almost hoping to evoke jealousy in him. I am desperate to ignite some sort of emotion in him, to engage him somehow. He'll see the photos we've taken at home, Sheila's slender arms wrapped around me, and he'll make comments, naming me a "ladies' man," a sort of hero. I'll hate him for this and wish to myself that it were the arms of good, strong men around me in the photos, men who laugh and feel and speak and love.

❖

Outdoors, we neaten the backyard over Thanksgiving vacation, grouping dead leaves with gentle motions across the earth. I am nineteen. This semester I'm learning to weld metal rods, to paint with oils, and to be my own unconditional back tickle. Even though I'm looking forward to meeting the right guy to share that job with me.

Zoe, now twelve, has just layered her hair. In her striped hat and gloves, she looks as though she'd fit on the side of an autumn shopping bag. She laughs when I tell her so, as I take her picture. "I'm so lucky to have a gay brother," she sings, implying a stereotype that a melting heart can forgive from a little sister. Julie wears the hand-me-down windbreaker of an old family friend. She remains soberly focused on the raking. Inside, my mother stacks the clean dishes as my father settles at the bay window with a draft of my philosophy paper. He lowers his spectacles, looking for strength and security in the Times New Roman of his son's ideas. He has not always known enough of his own strength to meet this son's eyes, to know him. But something in him has been defrosting ever since he found out that his son too was a prisoner. Though the exposed absence of our relationship has alarmed him, it's colored his once-smirking eyes with a new earnestness. He wants to understand, and he's almost there. We're almost there together.

The grass is still new, baby hair in clumps of wet dirt. Even Julie admits the effort is futile: "I feel dumb working so hard to get these leaves off. This grass isn't going to last the winter, anyway." Still we move across the yard, stroking it softly with our rakes, tickling the ground. In these moments my lips will part, tap each other affectionately, like old friends, and communicate a feeling. "I guess we want a clean lawn when the snow melts this spring," I offer. "A lawn free of autumn decay," I add, grinning like a playful poet. Julie rolls her eyes and smiles sheepishly. Feeling warm, I lick my lips. They are learning, I hope, to speak again.

FIGHTING FOR LIES
AIMEE LUKES

Billie was studying at Alaina's house. She was trying to avoid thinking about Spanish by figuring out Christmas gifts before New Year's rolled around. (Billie's mother always made jokes about her late Christmas shopping.) She was also using it to avoid thinking about kissing Alaina. If the thought got stuck in her head, she wouldn't be able to think of anything else until she did it. Even though she had a boyfriend. Instead of kissing her, Billie stole Alaina's glasses.

"Hey! What are you doing?" Alaina was obviously surprised. "No fair!"

Billie put them on. "Wow, Laney, you're fucking blind."

"Am not!"

"Okay, maybe it's not *that* bad."

"Give them back, Billie."

She cocked a smile. "Okay, fine. Just let me put them back on you."

"Really?" Alaina didn't sound impressed.

"Yes." Very carefully, Billie held out the glasses.

"Don't poke me in the eye."

Billie squinted. "I won't!" It was a bit difficult to get them over the ears properly, and Alaina had to readjust them, but Billie managed to get them on.

"Did they bother you at first?" she asked. "When you started wearing glasses, I mean."

"I kept forgetting them at breakfast, but my mother would always catch me before I walked out the door," Alaina told her.

"I bet that was a load of work." Billie sighed and lay back. She snuck her hand down to grab Alaina's. Alaina looked surprised for a minute, like she wasn't sure what Billie was going to do, but that passed when Billie did nothing. She just wanted to hold her hand. She couldn't do the other things she wanted—things that ranged from raunchy to sweet, but all were intimate.

I promised I would stop doing this. She was supposed to stop being so affectionate, as if starving those desires could make them die. She couldn't help it, though, and she kept being overly affectionate to cover just how much she touched Alaina. She had the worst urge to pull down Alaina's blouse and kiss her shoulder. Billie's finger twitched. *I could use a cigarette.*

"Are you coming drinking with us on Saturday?" she asked. "To the airport."

"Do I have a choice?" Alaina joked.

"You're the captain," Billie told her. That nickname, born in a childish game of pirates, wasn't used often, but it was always used affectionately. "Would you like another lesson in how to be bad?"

"Will there be boys there?"

"We weren't really planning on it, but we can invite some." Billie refused to frown.

"A girls' night sounds nice."

Billie grinned. "Good." There was a dip just above

Alaina's collarbone that Billie wanted to lick. She wondered what Alaina's skin tasted like—perfume? lotion? salt? *Books*, she decided. She shivered when she imagined her mouth on Alaina's collarbone, her tongue teasing the skin there. She let go of Alaina's hand.

❖

Alaina sat in the circle between Gayle and Barbara, across from Billie. There was a bottle of rum in the center, and Barbara's chubby ankles nearly touched the base. She was the tallest, and it didn't help that she had scooted in closer than everyone else. Gayle's ankles, by contrast, were bony, almost refusing to match the rest of Gayle's body (save for her thin, elegant fingers). Alaina's feet were flat and wide, and her heels jutted out a bit oddly, in her opinion. Billie's were small and smooth, and her ankles were delicate bumps that were almost invisible in the night.

Alaina reached for the rum, but Gayle got there first, so Alaina flopped onto the ground. It was disorienting to stare at the night sky, and she couldn't recognize any of the constellations, try as she might. She didn't know if she had drunk too much or if she was just shitty at astronomy. She hummed a little tune, but she didn't know what she was humming.

Barbara burst into titters.

"What?" Gayle asked, placing the rum back in the middle of their lopsided circle.

"Alaina," Barbara told her, finally stopping. "She is so out of it tonight."

Billie only stuck her tongue out and made farting noises in Barbie's direction.

"Stop that," Barb told her.

"Yes, Barb." She fidgeted a bit while Alaina continued to hum away the silence. "Don't you think," Billie cut in, "that we should turn the headlights on? It's really dark now."

"Yeah," Gayle agreed. "We don't want people sneaking up on us."

"Nah," Alaina told them. "It's too late in the season for that."

Barbara fell into a fit of giggles again. "What season is that, *boy* season?" This time the other girls giggled with her, and Alaina swung herself up to get the rum. This time, she beat Billie.

"You want it?" Alaina asked, sloshing the bottle.

"Yes!" Billie answered, probably more loudly than she intended.

Alaina laughed. "Rum for the captain first." She took a quick swig, then handed it over.

"I like rum," Billie said needlessly. Barbara patted her on the back while she drank deeply. She cradled the bottle in her arms. "I think I love it more than I love babies."

"Let's put the rum back, Billie," Gayle said, slipping the drink from her arms. "The boys will show up soon."

"Oh, great," she groaned. "Show up just when we're *blind drunk.*"

"When else?" Barbara said. Her laugh was more like a set of hoots, and Alaina couldn't stop giggling until Gayle shushed her repeatedly.

"They're coming, they're coming," Billie whispered.

Each boy was driving his own car, and it took Alaina a few minutes to remember that they probably wanted some private time with their girlfriends. They stopped a few feet away, still in the airport's clearing. Alaina was thinking about how cool it was that abandoned air fields had *so much room* when Gayle hauled her to her feet.

"Jeremy, you know Alaina," she was saying.

"Hi, Jeremy."

Jeremy shot her a shy smile. Christopher, Billie's boyfriend, elbowed Jeremy. Their eyes met, and Chris gave Jeremy an encouraging nod. "Hey, Alaina." He cleared his throat. "I'm glad you're here."

Suddenly, all her friends were gone, and it was just her and Jeremy.

"It's kind of cold out here."

"Well, it's November."

It was Alaina's turn to clear her throat, and she stared down at her feet.

"Oh, right! Um. Do you want to go back to my car? We can warm up in there."

Alaina smiled. "That would be lovely, Jeremy."

Jeremy looked very surprised when Alaina kissed him in the backseat. Alaina was wondering where to put her hands as he kissed her. He stroked her hair—something she wasn't particularly fond of—and whispered how she was really sweet and he found her smile endearing. So she smiled. It turned out that she didn't have to worry about where to put her hands. Jeremy seemed perfectly fine holding them while they kissed, softly rubbing her wrists with his thumb.

Everything was wrong, but Alaina didn't care to say that. She wasn't going to date him again, that was for sure, so there wasn't a problem with letting him have his one night of kissing, was there? She'd have to ask Billie about that later. Some time when she wasn't focused on how to move her tongue.

❖

They were in Billie's backyard. There was snow on the ground but not very much under the tree. Billie was smoking, but she was almost down to the butt. She'd offered Alaina a cigarette, but Alaina declined.

"So how was Jeremy?" she asked. "You never told me."

Alaina stuck her tongue out. "He was all wrong," she explained. "I guess...there wasn't anything *wrong* with his technique—though I could use some practice, I suppose—but I just didn't like it."

"Well, how do you like to be kissed?" Billie asked.

"I don't know!" Alaina giggled. "I just...I don't know if I want to keep being the third wheel."

"You'll find someone," Billie assured her.

"I don't *want* someone," Alaina insisted. She became very quiet and leaned against the tree. "Doing all this stuff—drinking and smoking and boys and skipping class—I'm not built for it, Billie."

"What are you saying?" she asked.

"I feel like I'm being pressured to do those things. That isn't right, Billie."

Billie flicked her cigarette to the ground and stomped it out. "I'm sorry, Captain. I'll tell the girls to back off."

"It's okay...I should have said something earlier."

Billie cleared her throat. "So, did you hear the news?"

"What?"

"Barbara and Melvin are having sex."

Alaina's face turned red faster than a stoplight, and Billie laughed.

"I'm kind of jealous," Billie admitted. "I mean, it's been so long for me...and Christopher's still not ready. Or maybe he just thinks *we're* not ready."

"I...What is sex like?" Alaina asked.

Billie paused to consider. "Filling."

"What?" Alaina shrieked.

"Well, what else would it be?"

"Loving? Romantic?"

"I wanted to pick something that was more...universal."

"And is it still universal if you don't have a penis?" Alaina blurted out before covering her mouth.

"Not so hard to say, is it?"

They both giggled, and Billie reached down to hold Alaina's hand. She leaned back next to Alaina on the tree. They turned their heads to look at each other, and Billie wanted to kiss her. She smiled to cover it up, and Alaina smiled back nervously.

Why should she be nervous? And then it hit her. *She wants to kiss me, too.* There was no time to think; Billie just leaned in.

Alaina didn't taste like books. If softness had a taste, it would have tasted like Alaina. The Chapstick on her lips had dried out, leaving them slightly raw. Her mouth was a little on the wide side, and she was sloppy from inexperience, but she compensated by letting Billie lead.

For Billie, it lasted forever and ended too quickly. When she pulled back, she saw the most scared look on Alaina's face.

"I'm s-sorry," Billie stammered. "I shouldn't have...It was stupid. I—I thought...I thought you wanted me to kiss you."

"I do."

Thank God it's not just me, she thought. Her heart was still fluttering, and it wasn't just from kissing. Billie was scared, too.

They stood there, shivering or shaking, Billie couldn't be sure, until Alaina spoke up.

"Can I kiss you again?"

Billie nodded, and Alaina pulled herself up to kiss her best friend.

❖

This is bad. No, this is worse *than bad.* Billie had refused to leave her room since Alaina left. She'd skipped dinner because she couldn't bear to look at her parents. How could she talk to them and pretend she hadn't kissed another girl? She was so scared she'd blurt it out, so scared of what would happen if she told them…but how could they not see it? It was all she could think about.

She didn't have the strength to cry, and she wondered if Alaina was crying. Did Alaina manage to eat dinner? She could imagine Alaina's nervous smile, her stuttered body language, her shifting attempts to hide her feelings.

Billie felt empty. The elation she had when she realized Alaina wanted to kiss her had given way to fear and shame, which Billie had wrestled with. Now she was hollow. Her mind couldn't produce emotion; it could barely create thought out of the string of nothing that encased her. She knew she wouldn't feel that way when she woke up, but she couldn't get to sleep. She was restless. Her mind buzzed; thoughts chased each other like a dog chased after its tail. She knew it was pointless, but that didn't mean she could stop it.

It was late at night when she snuck into the kitchen. When she opened the fridge, there was a plate for her wrapped in aluminum foil. She slid it into the oven, hoping it wouldn't be too long until the food was hot. She was famished. She was pouring herself milk and fetching a fork when the lights turned on.

"Hello, sweetie," Mary Alice said.

Billie took a deep breath. "Hey."

"I knew you'd be hungry."

"I can see that."

Her mother chuckled. "It's pork chops, you know. Mashed potatoes and green beans, too. I know how you like green beans."

"Thanks, Mom." Billie sat at the table. "What are you doing up so late?"

"I heard you rummaging around." Mary Alice rested her chin in her palm. "What's wrong, baby? Did you and Alaina get in a fight?"

Billie hadn't thought of a way to explain why she'd locked herself in her room, so she was glad that her mother had provided her with one. She nodded, and her mother reached over and pulled Billie's head to her chest.

"Everyone fights, you know. You two will make up soon."

"She's just jealous of Chris. She can't find a boy she likes, and she blames us for picking out boys she won't like." The jealousy part was probably true, Billie realized, though she couldn't imagine anyone as docile as Alaina being jealous.

"She'll find someone," Mary Alice said immediately. "You have to understand, Billie, it must be hard to come here and find friends who all have nice boys. Alaina hasn't had a boyfriend before. Maybe she feels like something's wrong with her, so she's lashing out at you to work through those feelings."

"I know she's more responsible than me—"

"You're doing fine, sweetheart."

"—but sometimes she can be so immature." Billie pulled her plate out of the oven and set it down at her seat.

"Alaina is a good girl, Billie. She'll apologize and explain, I'm sure of it. When she does, I want you to forgive her. Right away, too. You don't want poison in your friendship." Mary Alice squeezed Billie's arm. "Besides, forgiveness is good for the soul."

When she went back to her room, Billie didn't have a problem getting to sleep.

❖

Tuesday morning, Billie spent her time trying to figure out how to act around Alaina. Would Gayle and Barbara take it amiss if she wasn't happy and affectionate? Would Chris? She wasn't sure she could touch Alaina, not now that she knew… But she couldn't be affectionate with Gayle and Barbara and then ignore Alaina, could she? The fighting excuse would work again, but Billie hadn't told Alaina, and if Alaina thought Billie was mad at her…

She definitely wanted to kiss Alaina again, and if Alaina thought Billie was mad at her because they'd kissed, then it probably wouldn't happen. *It's wrong. Fuck it; I'm wrong.*

It turned out that it didn't matter; Alaina was avoiding Billie.

Billie decided that was good. She told herself that one of them had to have self-control. Every time she saw Alaina turn away from her, she reminded herself that they were both sick. It was a whisper in her head: *If you don't want anyone to find out, don't do it.* Her father had told her that when she was six. She'd called her cousin stupid on Christmas Eve and earned two spanks with three minutes in time-out.

Billie skipped Home Ec to go home. She snuck through

the back door and down the hallway to get to her room. The minute she hit her bed, everything gushed out of her. She sobbed into her pillow, trying to muffle the sound. It wasn't long before the whole top of it was wet, but she didn't bother turning it over. Her mother convinced her to eat dinner with the family, but she mostly played with her food. She didn't have an appetite.

"Are you still fighting with Alaina, sweetheart?" Mary Alice asked.

Billie nodded. "I told Chris that maybe we could find her a boy that's more her type," she said, "and he got mad at me because she didn't like the last two boys."

Mary Alice sighed, and her husband, Harold, shook his head.

"Boys shouldn't insult their girlfriend's friends. It isn't classy," he told her.

"Of course it isn't, Dad."

Back in her room, Billie avoided looking at the box surrounding her curtain rod and went to her closet. On a high shelf rested a stuffed rabbit. She held it to her chest and pulled her blankets all around her.

"You still love me, don't you, Babbit?" she asked.

The threadbare bunny didn't answer, but Billie still felt comforted. She rested her head on top of the rabbit's. It smelled like her mother's perfume, despite having been in the closet for several months. Now all she had to do was find a way to make her heart stop hurting.

"This is going to be hard, isn't it, Babbit?"

The rabbit still didn't answer, but Billie remembered what her mother always said: "The best friends don't have to talk to make you feel better."

❖

Alaina touched her lips for what must have been the thirtieth time that day. Each time she did, it was like an echo of how Billie's mouth had felt on hers. She was supposed to be vacuuming the living room, which she was glad for. She needed the time to think, and she hated not having anything to do with her hands. That morning, she had wondered if Billie would be angry with her or if Billie liked the way she kissed her. Every time she saw Billie at school, her stomach twisted in knots, She couldn't remember how to act normal anymore, all she could think was that she had to get away. She was scared of someone finding out, but she was even more scared of kissing Billie again. She was afraid Billie would hug her or squeeze her shoulder or hold her hand like she usually did, and maybe Alaina would read too much into it, or maybe Alaina would let something slip…or maybe the way she felt would get worse.

Kissing was the first step, wasn't it? Then there would be tongues and taking clothes off, and that was wrong. Thinking about it didn't feel wrong; in fact, thinking about being naked with Billie didn't make Alaina feel anything. She wanted so badly to be normal, but if she kept kissing Billie, she was afraid that she would feel something. If liking girls was a sickness like everyone said, then it could get worse. It would be irresponsible to let that happen…*and it would break my parents' hearts.* Her parents would get her help, of course, but they might lose their family money.

Alaina wasn't sure if she was more scared of disappointing her parents or being sent to a facility. She'd heard whispers of what went down in those places: People would yell at you and beat you; they would strip you naked and make you look at naked pictures, then make you sick. But Alaina heard other whispers, whispers that said homosexuality was natural.

They're only whispers. If they had any merit, we'd know them as the truth, wouldn't we? God would know it as the truth, and it would be in the Good Book.

Alaina unplugged the vacuum and started wrapping up the cord. She was going to sweep the kitchen next, even though she hadn't been asked.

❖

Tap, tap, tap. Alaina rubbed her eyes. Her clock said it was almost five in the morning. *Tap, tap tap.* It was just starting to get light out, and Alaina peeked between her curtains to see Billie staring down at her.

"What do you want?" Alaina asked, bewildered.

"Let me in!" Billie hissed.

Alaina opened the window, but she wouldn't let Billie climb in. "What are you doing here?"

"You can't pray me away," Billie told her angrily. "I'm not some demon set out to plague you, all right?" She looked at the ground. "I just like you, that's all."

"You can't like me."

"Why? Because you're a bookworm and I'm the belle of the ball?" She smiled at her joke, but Alaina didn't laugh, and the smile faded. She shuffled her foot, shifting snow around. "It isn't fair," she finally said.

"It's just better this way," Alaina said. "For both of us."

Billie spat on the ground. "That's a lie! You can make a decision for yourself, but don't you pretend that you're doing something for me just because you're scared! I'll make my own decisions, and if—if you don't want me to kiss you, I won't. But don't tell me you're doing it for me. You're not." She was rubbing her hands together, and Alaina thought Billie looked more like her than she ever had before.

"I do want to kiss you again."

"But you won't, will you?" Billie asked.

"Just once," Alaina promised. "Like a good-bye kiss. We won't do it again afterward." She leaned out the window, and Billie kissed her. Billie's lips were dry from the cold, but Alaina was still surprised at how warm she was. Their hands were next to each other on the windowsill, and Alaina didn't even notice how scratchy Billie's yellow gloves were.

And then it was over.

"So that's it," Billie said, her breath clouding up between them.

That's it. Alaina couldn't stand that thought, so she grasped Billie by the shoulders and pulled her in for another kiss.

Their cold breath mingled together in the air, and they stood, foreheads touching, looking at each other, neither sure what to do. Billie spoke first.

"I'm tired of fighting." She sniffed. "I'm tired of fighting myself, I mean. It's awful."

"I can't stop," Alaina said, betraying her hopelessness with her tone. "I have to try to be good. I just have to. We're supposed to honor our parents, and if I can save them some heartbreak, then I will."

"I've been trying that," Billie said, "and it's brought me nothing but misery."

Alaina grinned. "That's why we're completely different people. And so are our parents."

Billie stepped back. "They want the same thing, Captain.

And you'll end up destroying yourself before you can give it to them—trust me, I know!"

She didn't look away from Billie, but she didn't say anything, either. Billie stared back at her, then shook her head and left.

I don't need your approval, Alaina thought. She wanted to shout after her, but she knew her parents would hear. She kept silent.

There Was a Knocking on the Door
Andrew Arslan

The silence of the car ride from the grocery store was begging to be broken, but every time I opened my mouth nothing would come out. I felt muted by uncertainty, not knowing what his reaction to my revelation would be. I had heard enough horror stories on the news—the barrage of teen suicides, and the mere fact of the Ali Forney Center for homeless gay youth's existence, were a daily dose of reality. Being gay isn't all that easy, even in New York. There were so many things that I had heard or read that encouraged me to stay closeted, to keep this secret to myself, to let it slowly eat away at everything in my life and leave me miserable. Other times I would hear a story that would fill me with hope. Hope is all I have to help me come out.

My father is Muslim, and that had always crossed my mind whenever I thought about coming out to my parents. He had always spoken to me about treating everyone fairly, with respect, and gay folks were surprisingly never an asterisk; they were never an exception to his beliefs. I took comfort in his words of support, and it had prepared me for this very moment. So why was I so scared? Opening my mouth seemed so difficult, and to speak was beyond impossible. Anxiety was getting the best of me as I contemplated whether or not tonight was the night.

I continued to tell myself that I would just come out with it when we reached a specific street corner, and every time we passed it I would go on to tell myself that it would be the next one, and then the next one. I finally decided that I would just come out with it once we went over the railroad tracks, which would probably be the safest time to do it as well. My father wouldn't be able to just stop dead on the tracks should it be such a shock to him. As we went over the tracks my body tensed up, my heartbeat increased, and my palms began to sweat.

"I'm gay," I said as I felt the back of my neck begin to heat up.

"What?" my father asked in an extremely shocked tone.

"I'm gay," I repeated nervously.

"I can't believe this," he said.

He couldn't believe it? I thought I was becoming too obvious. Do I not sound it? My brother says I look like I am, too.

"Are you mad?" I asked to absolute silence.

He continued to drive up the avenue and then made a right on our block. I was beginning to feel sick and starting to wonder if I had made a mistake coming out to him. He pulled into the driveway and turned the car off. He sat there motionless for what seemed like an eternity. Thinking that he would be okay with it was already beginning to seem foolish. He didn't want this to be true for his son. This situation wasn't playing out as I had hoped. Finally, he asked, "You don't like girls?"

"No," I said softly, unsure of what was going through my father's mind.

"Do you want to become a girl?" he asked me.

I couldn't believe that he had asked me that. Was my father really this ignorant?

"No, I don't want to become a woman," I said, sounding annoyed by his question.

"I can't believe this," he said as he opened the car door to get out.

I also got out of the car to follow him into the house, where I was sure things would quickly go downhill. I hadn't known what to expect, and now I didn't know what to make of his disbelief. I didn't even know what I'd wanted to hear. Would an "okay" have been good enough? Had I been expecting a happy ending, and for everything to turn out wonderfully? Where was my well-known pessimism?

I had no idea what was going to happen once we got inside. This entire moment had quickly become everything I'd dreaded about the idea of coming out. My father wasn't as open-minded as he made himself look. He was beginning to sound like the typical father you hear about that doesn't want a gay son. Was I just overreacting in my mind without giving him time to accept it? Should he need time to accept it?

"I can't believe this," he said again. "It's such a shock. Can you change?"

"Change? No, I can't," I responded firmly as I closed the kitchen door.

"It's disgusting," he said as he turned away from me.

As I heard my father say being gay is disgusting, I felt more than just hurt. I felt betrayed. I couldn't believe that my father had just called it disgusting. He called me disgusting. Everything he had ever preached about treating gay people fairly was just shit. He didn't mean any of it. Everything at that moment seemed like a lie. Was I going to lose my father over my coming out? This new label completely changed his feelings toward me. It revealed my father's hypocrisy and how weak his love for me was.

My mom walked into the kitchen, unaware of what was going. My father still stood with his back to me as he looked toward my mother. She immediately realized that there was tension in the room.

"What's going on?" she asked.

"I'm gay," I responded.

"I knew that already," she quipped.

"How?" my father asked my mom.

"I saw papers in his room from politicians about gay marriage."

"Don't you want to have kids?" he asked me as he turned around to face me.

"I can still have kids," I said as I realized that my father really didn't know that much about gay people. He was obviously just like many others who assumed that gay people couldn't have kids. My father was lost in his own ignorance on the topic. *I shouldn't have to go through this*, I thought. I shouldn't have to educate my own father on a subject he used to frequently talk about supportively. Why did everything have to change because I'm his son?

"I can't believe this," my father said once again as he left the kitchen.

As I began to walk away from my mother, completely distraught over what had just happened, I heard her say, "You shouldn't have told him." I didn't care enough about her statement to respond to it. What was done was done and there was no changing it. Why shouldn't I have told my own father?

I walked past his room and went up to my bedroom to lie facedown on my bed. I pressed my face deep into my pillow, wanting to scream. Then I heard footsteps coming up the stairs. There was a knock on the door. It was my mother.

She welcomed herself into my room without a word to me and closed the door. She sat down on my bed and looked me straight in the eyes. I knew she was about to lecture me on how I shouldn't have told my father, but I didn't want to hear any of it. I didn't care what her reasons were. I had done what I wanted to do even if the outcome wasn't what I was expecting.

"You're stupid for telling him. You're really stupid."

Stupid? How could my mother call me stupid for coming out to my father? I felt attacked for opening up to them about my being gay. She always complained that I didn't talk to my father enough, or that I didn't talk about myself enough, and now that I had done just that, it was a reason to call me stupid.

"Why didn't you tell me first?" she asked.

"Because I knew you wouldn't care if I was."

"You should have just told me. I would have told you not to tell him."

"I would have told him anyway, and it's already done, so I don't know why you're telling me this."

"Because you're stupid! You shouldn't have opened up your mouth without talking to me first!"

"How am I stupid? Either way I would have told him, regardless of whether you told me to tell him or not. It was either I tell you both or I tell neither of you," I said as I got off the bed.

"You're stupid because he's Muslim! He doesn't think like me! You should know this!"

"Can you stop yelling at me?"

"No! You're so stupid! I can't believe you told him this!"

I began to feel a tightening in my throat as I grew tense in my mother's presence. I wanted to start crying so badly, but I couldn't break down with my mother in the room. I didn't want to stand there or be near her any longer as she continued to attack me.

"Get out of my room. I don't need you to do this to me right now."

"You're selfish. You're selfish, and that's all you are," she said.

"No, I'm not."

"You're stupid and selfish. You didn't have to tell him, and you did because you're selfish."

"Get out of my room!" I yelled back at her.

"You're selfish," she said one last time as she walked out of my room. I walked over to the door to slam it shut and lock it. I didn't want her to come back in again. I didn't want to hear anything else that she had to say. I didn't want my decision to come out to my father to be attacked and to be labeled as stupid. I felt as if I had done the right thing. I knew I'd done the right thing. I didn't want to be someone who lied to his parents for the rest of his life. I didn't want to stay in the closet around my friends, so why should I stay in it for my family? Why should this one thing change so much? How could something so small have such a huge impact on how others perceived you? Would they decide it was worth losing me over? Was it worth losing them over?

I got back under my covers and pulled the blanket over my head. How was I selfish? How could I be called selfish? Weren't they selfish? I could be out doing drugs or committing crimes. I could get a girl pregnant, but no, I'm gay, and that's the worst thing that could possibly happen. I'm the first person in my family that's going to go to college, but my being gay needs to change. My family is rejecting me for opening up. They are the ones telling me that who I am needs to be changed, or that I should have kept it to myself. Hypocrites. Who is my mom to call me selfish? Just because she doesn't want to deal with my unhappy father, I'm suddenly selfish? I thought that's what married couples do—deal with each other.

My throat began to tighten again, but this time I had to let it all go. I released all of the pain I was feeling. I tried to quiet my sobbing by pressing my face into my pillow. I felt my pillow slowly begin to stick to the skin around my eyes as it began to get wetter and wetter. It hurt to cry, but I needed to.

How could I be so stupid as to think that my father would react to this with nothing but pure acceptance? How could I be so ignorant? Every time he spoke positively of gay people, I should have realized that didn't include me. I should have known better than to pretend that things would work out no matter what. Thanks to his liberal sympathies, for the first time in my life I had begun to see things in a positive light. I'd thought I could be myself—that when I came out, he would accept me. Now I realized that my pessimism had always prepared me for the worst. Had I expected things to go terribly wrong, I probably would have been stronger than this. I wouldn't be this mess, sobbing like a child, clutching my pillow at the age of eighteen.

It was the first time in a while that I'd felt so alone dealing with my being gay. My friends had been supportive for years, but here I was alone again. It had always killed me to keep this from my parents and from my family. Maybe I should have waited a little longer. But why should I have to? Why should I hide this from my own family? Shouldn't they know who I am? Should they know?

"Stop it!"

The shrill cry pierced through my circling thoughts. My mother's voice, and she sounded panicked. Immediately, I jumped out of my bed to see what had happened. I quickly ran down the stairs to see my parents standing in the bathroom with pills scattered across the floor. The two of them looked at me and didn't say a word.

"What—"

"Just go back to your room," my mom in a voice soft with despair. "This is why you shouldn't have told him. Go back to your room."

My mother's voice killed me. She sounded so sad. The pills were scattered all over the bathroom floor. The scene didn't seem real to me. This only belonged in dramas on television. This didn't belong in my house—in my family.

"What happened? Tell me!"

"He tried to take a lot of the stupid sleeping pills! Now go back up! I told you, you shouldn't have opened your mouth! Go up!"

I stood there frozen, staring at the two of them in the bathroom. I couldn't believe what I had just heard. My father hated me. He was absolutely disgusted by me. His feelings were so extreme that a permanent escape was his only solution. I had almost killed my father by saying "I'm gay."

"Go away!" my mother yelled again.

"I'm sorry," I said softly before turning away to go back upstairs to my room.

I couldn't believe what I'd just heard. As I crawled back into my bed I began to cry again. My own selfishness had almost taken my father away. I had just nearly lost my father because I didn't take into consideration what his feelings about my being gay would be. All I had wanted was to be open about myself. I didn't want to feel as if I was lying anymore. I didn't think my parents wanted me to lie, but perhaps it was better to protect someone's feelings than to tell the truth? I wish this didn't have to be so difficult. How could I have known?

I wasn't sure what I was going to do after tonight. How was I supposed to look at my father tomorrow, or ever? Would he even look at me? Would he stop talking to me? What if he didn't even come home tomorrow because he tried to kill himself again? Was that even what he had intended to do in the bathroom? My mind was consumed by the worst possible outcomes.

I felt as if I had just made the biggest mistake of my life. I'd handled my coming out poorly, and now everything to come would most likely be the polar opposite of what I'd hoped to achieve. Everything that I had imagined for myself in the future seemed to remain an unattainable dream. What if my father wasn't there in the future to see my someday-family, my someday-children? That would devastate me.

I saw a flash illuminate my window, followed by a strong boom of thunder. I felt its intensity through my body. A summer thunderstorm was about to come rolling in. The rain began to pour.

There was a knocking on my door. It was my father.

MY AAHANA

ARIANA MONTOYA

"Rise and shine, Joanna. You have to get this room presentable. You have a roommate coming and I expect you to treat her well," Madame Beauclerc ordered, pulling my covers away and trying to rouse me from my sleep.

"Jo. How many times do I have to tell you? I'm Jo." I groaned, yanking the covers back and turning onto my stomach, trying to ignore the middle-aged dorm mother and French instructor. I hated that woman.

"That's a man's name. Now get up, Joanna!" she replied tersely, yanking the covers off me completely. Turning to her quiet favorite, who was lurking in the hallway about to rouse me for breakfast, her tone was exasperated. "Marlena, you deal with her!"

A half hour and a cup of coffee later, I was conscious enough to be aware that I had a new roommate. I was also extraordinarily angry about it.

"I can't believe some new girl shows up and I have to share my room!" I exploded, angrily throwing my things onto my "side" of the room. Every speck of me was being obliterated from that side. My photographs, band posters, knickknacks, every bit of me was being restricted to one side of the room that had been mine since I came here when I was fourteen.

"It's no fair! All three years, we've had an odd number, so this chick shows up and now I have to deal with her encroaching on my space."

Laughing at my anger, my best friend Marlena simply shook her head. The motion caused her brown curls to stir, releasing her trademark floral scent about my room. Her dark brown, faintly red-tinted eyes sparkled. She knew that smell alone could calm me. "You're being too critical, Jo. She might be a very nice girl. Besides, haven't you always wanted a live-in girlfriend?"

Not able to resist her teasing, I grinned a little. My secret was safe with her, as it always had been. "Oh, of course, my love. Why do you think I invite you over all the time?"

We both broke into giggles at that. We were sisters of the soul, never meant to be lovers, though it didn't stop her from dating my twin brother.

"Anyway, I should let you get your things settled. Don't kill the poor girl." Giving me one more smile, she departed.

Alone with my thoughts, I let out a sigh. If I had to share a room, I wished it would be with Marlena instead of with some strange girl who could find out my secrets and expose me to the rest of my all-female classmates. I didn't need that kind of hell. I didn't need to wind up like Lilly.

Soft knocking brought me out of my musings. "It's open!"

The door swung wide to reveal the single most beautiful girl I had ever seen. Her almond-shaped eyes shined with pure innocence, the amber color even more vivid and beautiful when coupled with her dark skin and black hair.

"Hello. I was told this would be my new room. My name is Aahana Vasuman." Her words were accented lightly, sounding as if she had been taught the language by a British instructor.

"Uh—" My tongue felt swollen and useless, and my eyes were glued to her beautiful visage.

Shifting uncomfortably, she stood in the doorway, still clutching her bags. "Perhaps I have the wrong room?"

"No!" The word came out too loud, too harsh, and she flinched at it. My face heated. "No, I mean, this is the right room. I'm sorry, you just…caught me off guard. You're stunning." There wasn't a hint of flirtation in my voice, just honesty. I moved to help her with her bags and the door behind her, leaving us alone together in my room. Our room.

Quite surprised by my words, she smiled gently at me. "Thank you. But I'm certain you have the same effect, with those eyes." Her praise caused my entire body to heat.

Glancing in the mirror, I shook my head. Her eyes were like molten amber. Mine were a calculating silver-gray. There was simply no comparison to me.

Appraising the room thoughtfully, she cocked her head to the side. "I take it you were not thrilled to have a roommate?"

My face turned bright pink, I'm sure, but I laughed. Oh, did I laugh! "I was pissed."

Her smile was filled with humor. "Well, Joanna, I promise not to be too much trouble. Madame Beauclerc already informed me that you've yet to have a roommate since your arrival freshman year."

"Ugh. That woman! I'm Jo. Just Jo." I smiled and offered my hand to her.

She looked surprised and awkwardly shook my hand. "Sorry. Still getting used to the customs. We don't shake hands much in India." She looked embarrassed, as if she was afraid to look foolish to me.

"Eh, don't worry about it. Come on, I'll show you around." I grabbed her arm and pulled her from the room, ready to give a tour. "Welcome to the academy—dumping grounds for all those who were too smart for their parents to handle, complete with a lovely Christian theme." I gestured to the statue of the Virgin Mary in the courtyard. It was technically not a Christian school, but a private one in a Christian place.

Looking around, her golden eyes seemed to dance with intrigue, clearly taking this all in. From the dormitories to the Southern backdrop, it was foreign to her, but interesting. "Dear Jo, would it be all right to ask where the library is?"

I nodded, swallowing thickly. Every expression she made captivated me. She was too beautiful for words. Too sweet, too smart, too much of everything…I couldn't help but love her.

❖

Like bells, her laughter rang through the air as she tugged at my hair. "Oh, dear Jo, how do you get into such things?" She was gently pulling all the ornamentation from my stiff blond hair, sprayed into place in the hours prior.

Had I been in a better mood, I might have smiled at her laughter. However, all I could do at that moment was wince. "She asked me to help her practice! I didn't know she meant practicing her hair-styling—"

"What won't you do for Marlena?" Shaking her head, Aahana smiled and pushed the hair ornaments to the side as she worked my hair itself, trying to get it to loosen up.

"Sit through another reality TV marathon," I replied with a shudder, knowing it would earn me more of her rich, feminine laughter.

As I expected, my words were rewarded by her sweet-sounding giggles as well as a fleeting brush of her fingers on my neck. She either didn't notice, or didn't want to know why, when I shivered slightly. "I swear, if John and you had been switched, you would be her boyfriend. You're so loyal. Even when your poor hair suffers." She continued to pull things out, finally backing up and grasping my arm to go to the sink and turn the water on warm.

Knowing what she wanted me to do, I bent, putting my head under the current of hot water as she poured shampoo into her hands. "Maybe I do all this as an excuse to get one of your hair treatments for free." My tone was light, joking. But deep down there was a sliver of truth. Her touch was irresistible.

More laughter spilled from her lips. "You're so funny, dear Jo." She slipped her hands into my hair, lathering it slowly as she massaged the suds into my hair and scalp.

Biting back a sound of pleasure, I closed my eyes. Her touch was wonderful, but it almost undid me when coupled with her little name for me. "Dear Jo." I had asked her about it once or twice, but she would simply smile and tell me I was a dear. From the beginning, she'd captivated me, and my reactions had only become intense in the past few months.

Every day, we ate breakfast together, went to see Marlena in the courtyard, attended class, and even meandered across the street to the boys' academy to see my twin. We were together so much, but it was normal, because she was my roommate. Just my roommate. My heart clenched.

"All right, all done!" she announced in a chipper way, smiling at me as she watched me wrap my hair in a towel.

Standing in front of her, so close we could be embracing, I felt an intense longing. I could lean down and kiss her. I could hold her in my arms. In the end, though, she would most likely reject me. I would be just like Lilly, heartbroken and ostracized by everyone.

Besides, even if she did return the kiss, she would never

be accepted at home. Her ailing grandmother would disinherit her and her father would be quick to follow. They were very traditional, and so was she. It would only serve to hurt her relationship with them.

It was too much. My heart was tied into her and her happiness far too much. And it hurt. God, did it hurt.

❖

Watching my pretty friend pace, I frowned. Her posture was so defeated. Sliding off my bed to move to her side, I massaged her shoulders as she was talking on the phone, wanting her to relax. She was so tense, and the yearly talent show would be starting in only an hour or so. Our last hurrah before the month of exam prep and then finals.

"Yes, Father. I understand, Father. Yes. Yes. I love you too, Father." When she hung up, her eyes met mine, all of her pre-show excitement having wilted away.

Wordlessly, I opened my arms and she began to sob into my shirt, the shaking of her body causing the bells and chimes on her outfit to ring throughout the room. The jangling sound was a mockery of the beautiful rhythm they normally had. "Shh, it will be okay. The fune—"

"No! No! It's not that. Grandma is still with us. But she made a change to her will. If I want my father to keep his inheritance, I must comply with her last requests…When I graduate, I must marry the son of a dear old friend of hers." Tears caressed her cheeks, her lips trembling.

My own heart shattered in my chest. "Aahana…" I wanted to brush her tears away, kiss her, tell her she could not marry him because I loved her. But I could not. I could not risk the little time we had left together, nor could I ask her to do something she herself would consider an act of betrayal. Instead, I released her when she pushed back a bit.

Drying her eyes, she walked to the mirror and cleaned her face up. "Regardless, the show must go on." She gave me a wan smile and I nodded.

That night, when the talent show closed with her act, I cried. She was so beautiful. Too beautiful. Music, ancient and mystical sounding, played as her hips moved in time. The bells on her skirt tinkled with every motion, keeping your attention even more focused on her movement. Her hands swam in the air, graceful and almost exotic. It was an art. She was moving, breathing art.

Marlena took my hand, squeezing as we watched. She didn't know the full story yet, but she sensed my pain and longing.

After the show, Aahana came to me, nervous. "Was I that terrible?" She was searching my still-somber face, looking for a trace of my usual self.

Shaking my head, I smiled. "You were entrancing, amazing—the most talented of the night. Makes me wish I had the rhythm to belly dance." The last part was said jokingly, a wink added for effect. Everyone knew I was too gawky and uncoordinated for that. In the end, that's who I was. Awkward, joking, even when I was shattered on the inside.

"You're a true friend, dear Jo." Her arms wound around me as she closed her eyes. "Maybe I can convince my father to fly you out for the ceremony?"

❖

Before I knew it, it was time to see her off. Finals had been taken, school was over. Now to say good-bye to the only girl I'd ever loved.

"Thank you for seeing me off, dear Jo." A smile graced her features. Breathtaking, lighting my world. She gave me a hug, leaning her head against my chest.

"I'll always be here for you." I let go, feeling tears in my eyes. "Now, go on. I don't want you to miss your flight!" I wiped my eyes furiously and stepped back.

Her features softened as she gazed up at me. "You may call me, anytime." She turned, finally going. She got only four yards before I couldn't take it.

"Aahana!" Desperation leaked into me as she turned her amber gaze on me. "Aahana, I…" The airport was crowded, and it seemed cheap to tell her then. Nothing would change. She would still be the dutiful daughter who'd marry for family. I would still be suffering from hopeless, unrequited love. Worse than any of this, she would turn her back on my words and I wouldn't even be able to cherish our time together. It would be a mark, a stain on the end of our friendship. "I looked up what your name means. It's true. It's so beautiful. Aahana, the first rays of the sun." That was as close to a confession as I knew I would get.

There was something in her eyes at that. Understanding? I will never know. She wiped her tears away. And without a word, she trudged on.

❖

Time has passed. Lovers have come and gone. When life just gets to be too much, I still cry to my soul sister and my twin. But she will always be my first love, my dawn. My Aahana.

First Time
Archer Darke

Dear Hayden,

> *Wear this and come to my parent's house tonight at 7 p.m. I'll be waiting for you.*

All my love, Grace

Hayden Terraciano blinked for several seconds, reread the note, and then glanced down at the tuxedo pantsuit that lay in the box it had come with. What mischief was Grace up to? Shrugging, she pulled the suit from its wrappings and studied it, wondering if it would fit. She undressed, pulled it onto her lithe frame, and studied herself in the mirror. Surprisingly, it was a perfect fit and hung just right from her lean but muscled shoulders. She ran a hand nervously through her short auburn hair, wondering what important event was about to happen. Why else would Grace want her to wear this?

After an hour-long commute from the college both she and Grace attended, and where they had first met just over a year ago, she made her way up the driveway of Grace's parents' house and stopped before the huge oak door with its antique lion head door knocker. She'd only been here a couple of times before. On the first occasion, she'd received a stern grilling from each of Grace's mothers on her intentions toward their daughter—the most nerve-wracking thirty minutes of her life. She and Grace had only been dating a few weeks by then, but she'd allayed her mothers' fears by explaining how much she loved Grace and how she'd spent almost a year loving her in secret and being nothing more than the best friend she could be until Grace had confessed her own feelings.

She was shaken from her musings by the click of the door lock as somebody opened it from the other side. It swung open to reveal Grace, a genuine, loving smile on her face that left Hayden momentarily breathless. Stunned, Hayden took in the slinky black dress that Grace was wearing like a second skin. The fabric clung to her body in all the right places and moved with a whisper as Grace took her hand and gently pulled her inside the house, closing the door behind them.

They stood in the hallway, each quietly studying the other, each rendered speechless by the beauty before her.

Grace Taylor had to hold her breath as she studied her longtime friend and only recent girlfriend. Hayden exuded both elegance and sex appeal in the tuxedo Grace had picked out, and it was all Grace could do not to swoon into a puddle at her feet. Her heart was beating nine to the dozen and her body felt warm all over. Hayden was looking at her with hunger and love in her eyes, which traveled the length of her body and back, feeling almost like a caress. She moved slowly, more from fear of falling than anything else, a nervous smile on her face.

Endeared and provoked into action, Hayden slipped an arm around her waist and pulled her close, kissing her deeply when their lips met.

"God, you're so perfect," she whispered huskily.

Grace blushed and leaned forward, lightly running her tongue over Hayden's earlobe. "There'll be more of *this*," she lightly nibbled the soft skin, "later."

It was Hayden's turn to blush at the heavily seductive words that promised so much. She gazed into Grace's expressive green eyes, looking hard for any uncertainty, but found only passion gazing back. Swallowing down the raw emotion welling up inside because of what Grace was willing to give her, Hayden glanced down the hallway.

"Isn't there some important meeting I have to get through first?" she asked, somewhat confused. Grace chuckled and shook her head.

"Nope, it's just us here. My parents have gone to our cabin in the mountains for the holidays," she explained as she led Hayden down the hallway and into the dining room, where Hayden had to stop and gasp at the sight before her. The room was dark but for the light cast by the candles that littered almost every surface. The flames flickered and danced in the light breeze that came from the open patio door, casting a warm and shimmering glow upon the dining table. This itself was covered in beautiful silverware, dishes and plates that waited patiently to be uncovered. Deep red rose petals littered the table amongst the plates, adding even further beauty to the display before her.

Hayden gazed around the room, dumbfounded. "You did all this just for me?" she whispered, looking at Grace with such love that it was hard for the other woman to focus on her words.

"I'd do all this again and more just for you, Hays," Grace replied. She gasped when Hayden pulled her close and kissed her again—deeply, lovingly. They broke apart moments later, each slightly breathless. Hayden glanced at the table. Watching her, Grace chuckled.

"I know, I'm wanting to skip dinner too." She adjusted Hayden's bow tie as she talked and then leaned close for a quick kiss. Hayden smiled at her, desire clearly written all over her face. She ran her hands up and down Grace's sides, the silky texture caressing her palms.

"You look breathtaking, and you've been to so much trouble, so I'm going to patiently wait and thoroughly enjoy dinner with you tonight." She led Grace over to the table and pulled out her seat before sitting herself and arranging her cutlery. She stopped when she saw Grace grinning at her.

"What?"

"I feel bad now because I didn't actually cook any of this," Grace replied, a mischievous glint in her eye, "It's actually all junk food." She started removing lids to expose an assortment of burgers, fries, and pizza. Hayden chuckled appreciatively.

"You know me so well."

❖

An hour later, after a pleasant meal and an even better conversation, they sat in companionable silence for a few minutes. Hayden sensed Grace's hesitancy and shifted her chair closer, a small smile on her lips.

"I'm nervous too. You know nothing has to happen tonight, don't you?" She caressed Grace's face as she talked, an action meant to soothe and reassure. Grace gazed at her with such love in her eyes that Hayden's heart melted and she fell in love all over again. Nothing ever had to happen if Grace didn't want it to; Hayden would never dream of taking something Grace wasn't ready to give.

"I want it to," Grace whispered, turning her face into Hayden's palm and kissing the soft skin there. Then she stopped suddenly and cast her gaze back to Hayden. "I mean, if you want to…"

Hayden was having trouble thinking about anything other than Grace's soft lips grazing her palm. When Grace's words finally registered, she flustered and blushed profusely, "I-I do."

And it was true. She'd wanted to make love to Grace for so long. She'd thought about it since the day she had fallen in love with the blond beauty, albeit guiltily most of the time. Her daydreams were never about her own satisfaction, but rather about sharing the ultimate intimacy with the girl she loved and about making Grace feel as if she was the most precious and treasured thing in Hayden's life.

She pulled Grace toward her and kissed her deeply, threading her fingers through blond tresses and pouring as much love and desire as she could into the kiss. She paused for breath and leaned her forehead against Grace's.

"You have no idea what you do to me," she whispered before Grace captured her lips again.

"Does it feel like your chest is going to explode with something that seems even bigger and more amazing than happiness?" At Hayden's shaky nod, Grace continued, "You do that to me too. Let's go upstairs."

Hayden chuckled quietly as Grace stood. "You make me crazy, you know."

Grace pulled Hayden to her feet. "I like making you crazy." When she nuzzled Hayden's cheek and kissed her sweetly, Hayden blushed.

Grace led Hayden upstairs by the hand, her heart beating faster with each step. Neither spoke as they moved quietly through the house. A flight of stairs at the end of the upper floor led them to the attic.

"Welcome to the Taylor getaway room."

The converted loft was the biggest bedroom Hayden had ever seen. It spanned the whole width and length of the house and was decorated modestly in deep dark blue tones. The king-sized bed at the far end seemed to beckon them forward, but for the moment, she contented herself with slipping her arms around Grace's waist.

"This place is amazing. *You* are amazing." She brushed her lips lightly over Grace's neck. Grace turned in Hayden's arms and kissed her, letting her tongue caress the soft lips before dipping inside to explore more.

"You're better than amazing," she replied, moving her kisses along Hayden's jaw while tugging her bow-tie loose with fumbling hands. Once she removed it, she pushed the jacket from Hayden's shoulders and pulled the shirt from her trousers, letting her hands trail underneath and up over Hayden's heated skin. She lightly grasped Hayden's sides and pulled until she felt her legs hit the bed. Hayden stopped her from falling backward with an arm around her waist.

"Wait," she murmured, running her hands in a caress over Grace's back and fiddling with the zipper until she had it pulled all the way down. Hesitantly, she peeled the dress over Grace's breasts and pushed the material down to gather at her waist, all the while watching Grace closely for any discomfort. Finding none, she slowly feasted her eyes on her lover's newly exposed body, sucking in a breath at the beauty that greeted her.

"You're so beautiful," she whispered before lowering Grace onto the bed.

Grace pulled her down and kissed her. Her own passion was rising with every second that passed. "*You're* beautiful, Hays," she replied, unbuttoning Hayden's shirt and kissing the newly exposed skin.

Hayden blushed, but the moment was short-lived as Grace's mouth closed over a rapidly hardening nipple. She gasped as she felt Grace's tongue circle and flick, and arched closer when she sucked lightly, as if testing how much and how little was good.

Hayden moaned her approval before pulling back to remove her shirt and grant Grace better access. She straddled Grace's thighs, sliding her hands up and over her hips and caressing her stomach before tentatively moving over her breasts. She felt the nipples in her palms harden like pebbles and had to fight not to hurry. She didn't want to frighten Grace with her rampant desires. She wanted to take this slowly. She felt Grace's heartbeat pick up speed as she flicked the nipples gently with her thumbs, and then Grace's hands were upon hers and urging her to press and roll more firmly.

"That feels so good, Hays."

She smiled and Hayden had to lean down and kiss her deeply, to show her how much she appreciated this gift she had been granted. "I could touch you forever and never get bored, Gracie."

Grace moaned at the words and quickly shed both her dress and underwear. Needing to feel Hayden's skin, she kissed her as she unbuttoned the tuxedo pants and slowly slipped her hand inside. When Grace's fingers met silk wetness, Hayden's hips jerked. Suddenly afraid, Grace halted.

"Did I hurt you? God, Hayden, I'm so sorry." She began to pull her hand away, but Hayden gripped her wrist.

"No, God, please, don't stop."

Her voice was husky with need, her eyes hazy with lust and love. Grace saw it, and her own need rose within her. She pushed at Hayden's trousers and boxers, urging them off until she too was naked. She paused to look at her, to take in this moment she was experiencing for the first time. Hayden gazed back at her, the love and want so obvious in her eyes that Grace's heart gave a jolt and she pressed her lips to Hayden's, trying to communicate all her feelings through that one action alone.

"I love you, Hays. So much." More confidently this time, she slid her hand between Hayden's thighs and sucked in a breath at the molten heat she found there. Hayden moaned into her shoulder as she circled and dipped her fingers experimentally, feeling her grow harder and wetter as she moved. Grace felt Hayden's lips move haltingly on her neck, as if her ministrations were affecting Hayden's ability to make the simplest movements.

"So good, Gracie. I need more, please," she rasped, and Grace was powerless to decline. Slowly, she pushed her middle fingers inside, feeling Hayden's velvety walls surround her. She gasped at the sensation. Hayden rocked against her involuntarily, setting a steady rhythm for Grace to match.

Hayden felt her orgasm approaching fast as Grace slid in and out of her. She clamped her mouth down on Grace's shoulder, sucking and licking the skin there as she tried desperately to hold off the tide of pleasure. When Grace's thumb began to pull her hood back and forth, she knew it was impossible. Her thighs trembled and her breathing quickened as the first wave crashed over her. Shuddering, she cried out and rode Grace's fingers deeper, jerking as another wave surfaced. She could feel herself squeezing Grace's fingers, and the sensation drove her over once again. Moments later, she collapsed on top of Grace and panted into her shoulder, the last remnants of her orgasm slowly leaving her body in small spasms.

Smiling, Grace caressed her back and kissed her temple, loving the sense of satisfaction that had washed over her as Hayden came.

"Was that...good?" she whispered a few minutes later, wondering if Hayden had fallen asleep in her arms. She felt her shudder and was confused until she realized she was laughing quietly.

"This was supposed to be about you," Hayden murmured into her shoulder, "and yet I'm the one in pieces here."

Grace smiled as she laced her fingers through Hayden's short hair and gently pulled her up for a long and languid kiss. It seemed like forever before they finally broke apart.

"It doesn't matter about that, Hays, just that we're together like this."

"But I wanted to show you how much I love you," Hayden murmured.

"And you did, Hays, by trusting me enough to touch you like that," Grace replied softly. And then she grinned. "Besides, we still have the rest of the week."

HELLA NERVOUS
REBEKAH WEATHERSPOON

I'd wanted to hook up with Oksana Gorinkov for a long time. Our junior year I decided to do something about it. We'd been in the same homeroom since sixth grade. After our teacher had her introduce herself on her first day—wait, let me fix that. *The minute she came into the room*, I was caught in her snare. I know, right? It sounds a little desperate, but she's that hot. Our little piece of Los Angeles was diverse on the color scale, but my school was pretty split between Latino, white, black, and Asian. There were, of course, a few mixed kids here and there, and the random kid from some country we'd heard about but were never able to locate on a map. Oksana was the most exotic of the exotic.

When she walked into homeroom that day, time stopped for everyone. Even our teacher regarded her like some precious prize. Her skin was the shade of iced coffee, liberal on the milk, but her eyes were green, and her long, curly hair was brown with natural streaks of blond. It was braided in pigtails that first day. She looked so sweet and innocent. I knew instantly every boy in our class would swallow his playground pride to be nice to her. And even though I'd been crushing on various girls here and there for as long as I could remember, she was the first girl who made my palms sweat. After that first day, most teachers didn't make her talk. She was still getting a hang of her English, but over time I picked up a few bits about her.

She was half-Russian and half-black. Now, after puberty had started in on all of us, she was tall, at least five-nine. She lived with her grandmother and she was shy as shit. She reminded me of one of those little animals. Like if I offered her a treat she'd check me out for a few minutes, cautious as hell until she decided to snatch it from me before she bolted to a safe corner. I had no interest in hurting her, of course. I didn't believe in cruelty to animals or smoking-hot chicks. I just wanted to break that shell a little.

Once we hit high school, she started modeling. I thought it was a rumor, but—thank God for the Internet—it was true. At first I wondered how someone so sheepish could be such a natural in front of the camera, but I realized it was the perfect job for her. She didn't have to say a word. Around that time, some older guy started picking her up after school. He seemed pretty good-looking from a distance, but something told me there wasn't anything going on between them. I'd find out at some point.

By the time I got up the nuts to talk to her, I'd settled well into my butchness. It was just Mom and me, and she had finally come to terms with the fact that soccer meant more to me than any amount of shopping on Melrose. I ran with a couple of the other "guys" on the soccer team and we did all right. Plenty of girls were curious enough to let us have at them, but it was Oksana who had officially grown roots up under my skin as the season came to a close. I don't know, maybe I was high off all of our wins, but when spring hit, I was feeling extra horny and brave. I needed a challenge.

Oksana had taken up with this clique of Russian-Jewish chicks led by this girl named Marni, but it seemed like that was only so Oksana didn't have to sit alone at lunch. And even at lunch she sat at the end of the table and only really spoke when spoken to. They didn't treat her like crap or anything, but she was just so damn shy. Getting her to talk seemed like it would take a shitload of effort, even for someone like Marni who always seemed to be flapping her lips.

I decided the direct approach was the best way to go—to shock her into a response. That morning, I sent Mom off to work and got to school early. I was the first one in homeroom, chatting up Mrs. Porter while I helped her staple some stuff for her first-period class. Oksana always sat in the row closest to the door, but in the seat all the way near the back. My assigned seat was right next to her. She came into the room, head down, bag over her shoulder, her history book pressed tightly against her chest. Her hair was in a braid and she wore loose cargo pants that hung off her hips centimeters away from being against the dress code. When she put down her book, her tight T-shirt revealed hard nipples. She didn't seem to notice how good she looked. I waited until she was comfortable in her seat and then I leaned over.

"You have a boyfriend?" I said quietly, letting a smile play across my lips. She froze, head still down. Brad Grover looked over his shoulder at us. He was just as shocked as Oksana.

"Me?" she squeaked.

"Yeah." I nodded like it was the only suitable way to start a conversation.

She swallowed and tucked a loose strand of hair behind her ear. Cute straight girl move, number 408. "No."

"Who's that guy who picks you up sometimes?"

She thought for a moment, picking at the corner of her book. "He's just my friend." Something in her tone said she was telling the truth, but this guy was special somehow.

"You sure?"

"Yeah." She nodded, biting her lip. "Scooter's more like a brother to me. Plus he's twenty-one. That's too old for me."

"You drive?" I asked after Mrs. Porter took attendance.

The bell rang, saving Oksana from answering. She grabbed her books and bolted for the door.

Brad Grover picked up his bag and turned to me with a chuckle. "Good luck."

I punched him playfully in the arm. "Thanks."

Oksana and I didn't have any classes together. Your language elective set your schedule, and even though we were in the same level math class, I took Spanish and Oksana took the one period of Portuguese being offered. But I saw her again at lunch. I watched her, half listening to what the guys were saying. Cara jabbed me in the arm.

"What?" I yelped.

"I asked you a question, dickhead. What are you staring at?" She followed my line of vision as she asked. "Oh. Really?"

"Nah. I'm just looking."

"Mmm-hmm." Cara didn't buy it. It didn't help that Oksana chose that moment to look in my direction. A delicate pink hit her cheeks and she quickly looked away.

"Just don't break her." Cara laughed. "I heard that one's fragile."

"From who?" I said with a hint of irrational anger. Just like her modeling career was common knowledge, everyone was under the impression that no one but that guy who picked Oksana up had come even close to getting with her.

"I'm just saying. She's fucking shy."

"The shy ones are the best ones," Jamie said with her mouth full of sandwich.

"I'm just looking," I replied, closing the conversation. Just looking for now.

The next day, Oksana wore a short skirt. She had legs for days. I stared at them as she shifted her Converse under the desk. I leaned over and put a paper flower I'd crafted on top of her history book. "So that guy. Does he *have* to pick you up?"

She shook her head. "No. I walk home when he's working." She picked up the flower and put it to her nose. She didn't inhale, but her eyes closed for a moment, and she was somewhere else. My mouth popped open. When she looked at me, I managed to get it to work again.

"You want to come over tomorrow?" I asked boldly. In front of me, Brad twitched.

"I have to watch my sister." She had a sister? This was new bit of information, but I didn't want to tackle that family shit yet. I had to get her over to my house first.

"How about—"

"I can come over on Thursday." She peeked up at me through her eyelashes.

"We're taking the bus. That okay?"

"She lived in the Soviet Union, dude. The bus must be like a Rolls-Royce to her," Brad teased.

I almost smacked him in the back of the head, but Oksana's lip picked up at the corner in a little smile. "Yeah, the bus is fine."

She bolted like usual as soon as the bell rang. At lunch she was right back over with Marni and her minions, doing her best not to look my way.

That night, I waited for Mom to get home before I ate dinner. We watched reruns of *Friends* and then I nudged her toward a shower and bed. She skipped the shower and was snoring before I finished the dishes. After, I spent a few minutes online. It only took a second to find some pictures of Oksana. She modeled bathing suits for some lame teen clothing line. I jacked off until I fell asleep.

When Oksana walked into homeroom on Thursday, I almost came in my pants. She'd dyed her hair all the way blond and straightened it. It looked good no matter how she wore it, but the shift in her look was just plain sexy. She was wearing an even shorter skirt, this microscopic pleated thing. Very schoolgirl, very porny. The whole class looked at her. The prissy bitches on the other side of the room started their whispers right away. Even Mrs. Porter looked twice. I started mopping up my drool. Oksana didn't say anything when she sat down.

I turned to the front of the room and managed to get my shit together while the morning announcements were shouted out overhead. Finally I looked back in her direction. I wanted to say something witty and complimentary, but the bell rang. If it wasn't for slow-ass Brad and Oksana's super long legs I would have caught up with her.

During lunch she was the center of attention. I ignored Cara's low whistle as I watched Marni fuss over Oksana's hair and her outfit.

"Still just looking?" Cara joked. I didn't answer.

After class Oksana met me by my locker. I had no idea she knew where my locker was, but she popped up at my side all packed up. I wasn't sure if she was exactly ready, though. I couldn't read her expression. She looked resigned, maybe? Almost a little scared or sad as she gazed at the floor. But when I nodded down the hall and said, "Let's go," she followed me without hesitation. We listened to some freshmen talking shit about their friends on the way to the bus stop. Once we were on the bus, she didn't say a thing. When we got off it was only a few blocks to my house. I told her and she nodded. She didn't say anything else until I unlocked the front door.

"Are your parents home?" she asked.

"Not until late."

"Oh."

"Let's go to my room."

"Okay."

She followed me down the hall, and when I opened the door to my bedroom, I let her look around. I turned on my TV and flopped down on my bed.

"I don't live too far from here," she said.

"Oh yeah?"

"Yeah. We're right over on Sweetzer."

"Shit, that's real close," I replied. Then I got to the point. "Do you like girls?"

Oksana ran her finger over the base of one of my soccer trophies. She didn't turn around so I started getting undressed. I knew she'd heard me kicking off my sneakers and unzipping my jeans, but she stayed put.

Finally she said, "I think so."

"Have you ever done anything with a girl?"

She shook her head. "No, I—you're not wearing underwear!"

I looked down at my body, laughing at the ghastly expression on her face. "Yes, I am." I still had my sports bra on too.

"I mean, you're wearing boxers. I—"

"They're more comfortable, but I don't think they would look good on you." She looked down, like she was analyzing her underwear. "Come sit over here." I sat down on the bed and waited for her to join me. She folded her hands in her lap.

I had no idea what to do. My crotch was telling me to jump her, but I seriously couldn't get a good read on what she was thinking or feeling.

"Do you want to be here?"

She nodded, then said quietly, "Yes."

"And you get why I asked you over?"

"Yes. I'm just, how do you guys say it, hella nervous."

I laughed as she did her best Valley girl voice. "Don't be hella nervous. We don't have to do anything, I just wanted to open the door." Fuck, the fact that I'd gotten her to talk was a small miracle. I deserved a genius grant for getting her into my bedroom.

"I want to do something," she replied, her voice sounding sweet and eager. "I just..." My hand on her thigh stopped her from finishing. Her skin was so soft and warm. She tensed at my touch, gazing down at my blunt fingertips, but I could tell by the way her breath skipped she didn't want me to stop.

"I like your hair like this."

She looked up and met my eyes. Hers were so green. "My baba—I mean my grandma gets itchy with hair dye every once in a while. I volunteered to be her guinea pig this time."

"It looks good." My fingers wandered a little higher up her leg. I flicked the edge of her skirt. "Did you wear this for me?"

She hesitated before she said, "Yes."

I kissed her. It was a little awkward at first. She wasn't a good kisser. She kept her lips pursed too tight and she didn't grasp the concept of head angling, but soon I stopped, and she let me give her some direction.

"Just relax. Relax your mouth. Here." I brought my hands up to touch her. "Even relax your shoulders."

"I'm sorry." She blushed, looking away.

"Don't be sorry and don't be nervous. This is supposed to be fun, so just have fun with it."

She stood suddenly and started shimmying out of her skirt. My throat was suddenly dry.

"Will you finger me?" she asked. "I've always wanted to do that."

"Uh…yeah. Come back over here." When she'd stripped down to nothing but a small pair of pink underwear, that's what she did.

With her lying beside me I was suddenly doubting my skills, but that didn't stop me. And her fears didn't stop Oksana from opening her legs for me either.

❖

"I should get home," Oksana said some time later.

"You want me to walk with you?"

"No. I'm okay." This was supposed to be casual so I didn't push. I pulled some clothes on though and walked her to the door.

"I'll see you tomorrow?" I said expectantly, like I was freaked that she'd transfer schools or something.

She nodded, keeping her eyes down. "Will you show me how to do stuff on you? I want to know what you like."

I almost passed out. Dry humping was my favorite pastime. I could definitely show her that. "Yeah, um…yeah. We can do that."

"Okay. Night." She kissed me quickly on the cheek, then bolted down the street.

This went on for two weeks, though the routine was nothing close to dull. We'd see each other at school. Sometimes I'd flirt with her in homeroom, even though she never really flirted back. I'd watch her with no subtlety whatsoever during lunch. That guy still picked her up from school, but a few times a week, after the final bell, she'd come home with me. She got a hang of the kissing, though nothing turned her on more than my dry-humping technique.

When we caught eyes between classes, she wouldn't smile, but she'd blush like crazy and I knew she was picturing the things we'd done the afternoon before. I know *I* was. I liked to tease her about it 'cause that just made her blush even more. The guys asked questions. They got the feeling something was up, but with Oksana I didn't want to kiss and tell. I respected her too much.

Mid-April, things changed. She was quiet until we got to the bus stop. Traffic was backed up. When she figured we'd be waiting a little while for the next bus, she pulled out a little notebook from her bag.

"You wanna see my baby sister?"

"Yeah." She opened the notepad, maybe a journal or something. None of the writing on the first page was in English, but there was a Polaroid taped to the inside cover. She was in the picture too, holding a little girl in her lap. It was crazy that that much pretty had been pumped into one family. "She's cute. What's her name?"

"Ekaterina." Each syllable rolled off her tongue. It was crazy hot. "I've been calling her Katty or Pooh. She's three."

"She looks just like you."

"No." She shook her head. "She's prettier."

Oksana was crazy, but I let her have it.

When we got back to my house, I made us a snack that we ate while we watched TV in the living room. I made the first move again and this time we ended up on the floor. She was shy at first, as usual, but she let me go down on her. When we finished, I could tell something was wrong.

"Is this all you want to do?" Oksana asked as she buttoned up her jeans.

"What do you mean?"

"Fool around."

She'd been over a handful of times. And each time I'd just been focused on getting her naked. We were strangers with benefits. I couldn't help how hot she was or how bad I wanted her. It never occurred to me that *she* would want more. The secrecy and the casual tone of our relationship seemed to suit her reserved nature. Then it clicked.

"You like me, don't you!" I said a little too loudly. It came out totally fucked up, like I'd been trying to play her from the beginning. After her eyes popped open wide with shock and embarrassment, she quickly grabbed for her shirt. I dashed to her side before she could slip it on.

"I like you," I said quickly. I was practically in love with her, but I wasn't going to say that out loud.

"Or you like hooking up with me?" She glared at me. It was the most direct eye contact we'd ever shared. She wasn't about to let me slick my way out of this one, but I didn't need a way out.

"I like you. The hooking up is nice too, but I actually like you."

"I like you too, but I want to hang out with you. Like how couples do. Like girlfriends maybe, with talking and going on dates with the fooling around. Maybe you could come over my house and help me babysit. We have to keep our clothes on, but we can hang out. Katty's a good kid."

"We can definitely do that," I replied. That was when I

realized I really did want to meet her sister. I wanted to spend more time with Oksana, period.

It was subtle, but she exhaled. "Okay. I better go."

"You want me to walk with you?"

She thought for a minute. "Yes."

The whole way, I held her hand. My palm was sweating, but she didn't seem to notice.

That night, I found a piece of paper half-crumpled and wedged in my Spanish book. I had no idea how long it had been there, but when I unfolded it, I found Oksana's phone number. *Just call before eleven* it said below her digits. Maybe that's why she finally asked. She'd given me her number maybe months ago and I hadn't done anything but mount her at every turn. I looked at the clock. It was 9:45.

I called her, of course, psyched that Oksana answered on the second ring and a little turned on that she purred out some sexy greeting in Russian instead of saying hello.

We stayed up all night talking.

The next day, Oksana actually talked to me in homeroom and she let me walk her to class. She didn't hesitate finding me in the lunchroom. She ignored the curious stares from the guys and plopped down beside me. I was in heaven until Marni made a direct line for our table.

"Hey?" Marni said, her hands on her hips.

Oksana looked up and smiled at her like nothing was out of place. "Hi."

"Um. Why are you sitting over here?"

"I wanted to sit with Tracy," Oksana replied before she took a bite of her sandwich.

"Why?" I hadn't ever seen someone so confused and a little offended. Marni's world was slowly tilting upside down.

I did my best not to laugh in her face. Under the table, I slid my hand into Oksana's lap. Marni saw.

Oksana turned her head up and looked Marni straight in the eye. "'Cause she's my girlfriend."

Marni's face fell off her fucking head. "Oh."

"I'll see you in class," Oksana said, giving her the official shove-off. I didn't bother hiding my asshole grin when Marni glanced at me. She flipped her brown hair over her shoulder and stormed back over to her clique.

"Trace?" Cara gasped across the table. "You're gay?"

"Shut up." I laughed, but I felt Oksana get all rigid beside me again.

"Was that okay?" she said quietly. She was so cute when she got all bashful. "I didn't just out you, did I?"

She was so sweet and considerate, she didn't realize how silly that sounded. The doctor who delivered me knew I was gay the minute I popped out. But I melted a little as she blushed and nibbled her lip a little more.

"I think you may have outed yourself, but don't worry about me. It's totally okay."

"Okay," she said with her slight smile. And then she moved a little closer to me.

CHILI POWDER
ANNA MEADOWS

Mamá never warned me how different it'd be in a *gringo* town. She dyed my hair the color of corn tortillas, cut me bangs like Zooey Deschanel, and taught me to use a curling iron, like that was all it took.

My first clue should've been all the blues in my closet, how nobody in Kendall wore them except at night. Back home, my jeans and my denim skirts looked like nothing, but here, all the denim made me stick out like I was going for Madonna circa "Don't Tell Me." Mamá wouldn't let me wear jeans after she caught me watching the music video on TV when I was four because she said Madonna could make anything slutty, even Levi's. I got all the way to seventh grade before she lifted the ban.

Las camisolas I wore under my jean jacket worked back home too. Hell, they even had lace along the edges, and that made them good enough to wear lipstick with. In the *gringo* town, though, in the middle of all those sweater sets and starched collars, they made me look *barata*, like I had on lingerie to go to church. It wasn't like the girls in Kendall never wore spaghetti straps, but there was something about the bright colors and splashy flower prints that made it okay, that made it look cute and tropical instead of cheap.

But cheap was pretty much how I looked anyway, with my bleached-out hair and eyebrows (*Mamá* said they had to match), my lipstick that feathered when the other girls' stayed glossy as the hood of a waxed car, and my new push-up bras that Mamá said all the *gringa* girls wore (they didn't; most of them were too bony to have any *chiches* to push up).

The worst was when I made the jokes about fags or queers, *los maricónes* or *los playos*, whatever you wanted to call them. Those cardigan girls and Dockers boys looked at me like I was mean and stupid and *inculta*. I thought they'd know I didn't mean nothing by it. Boys who did stuff with boys and girls who did stuff with girls had to make the jokes first so nobody else got the chance. Back home, I'd gotten called *la tortillera* every time anybody saw me getting out of Reyna Soccoro's backseat, my lipstick smeared, her belt half-buckled. Only thing to do was wave, or say, "Yeah, so what?" or curtsy like the Queen of fucking England if I had on the right skirt for it. It was how to get by, how to make sure nobody said nothing about me spending the night at Nikki Quintana's, or getting behind the back chemistry lab counter with Daniela Concepción. I learned early that if I made fun of myself first, it took the fun out of it for everyone else.

But in Kendall it meant getting iced out of every table and bleacher during lunch. Those *gallinas* and their boyfriends looked at me like I'd spit on the shrine of *la virgen* and her roses. Like they'd never said anything about *los mariquitas* in their whole twin-set life. I would've sat down anyway, just to get to them, but they might've henpecked me to death and broken their special diets just to eat me.

They never would've made it a year at my old school. Back home, if somebody's mother heard from anybody else's mother that her son was *una mariquita*, or worse, her daughter *una tortillera*—a pretty son was better than a daughter who wouldn't wear a dress—she would've rounded up the church ladies to cast out *el demonio*. Salt on the pilot light and readings from *Eclesiastés* and making you say the names of *los apóstoles* over and over until you can't remember your own, let alone some girl in a gray hoodie who smells like her brother's aftershave.

I wasn't sitting inside for lunch, though. Nobody but freshmen ate inside, and the dozen girls who thought Mr. Hemsley was so *guapo* they brought their Wonder Bread into the biology lab. Plus Mamá warned me it snows here in the winter, so I better get my time outside now before the whole world iced over. I found a spot under a tree so big and fluffy that with its leaves turned chili-colored, it looked like the biggest marigold. It cast a ring of shade that nobody else got near. They must've thought they'd catch the meanness.

I kept my head down, sprinkling chili powder on the orange Mamá had cut for me, as a boy in jeans and a zip-up sweatshirt crossed the grass. If I let my hair fall in my face I could watch him through my bangs. He was cute, the kind of cute I'd wanna do something with, and for me that was something, since guys had never "done it for me," like my *tío* would say.

Wasn't that I hated guys or anything, fish and bicycles and all that *mierda*. Sometimes at my old school I got behind the bleachers with one of them and let them touch my *chiches*, to be nice, so the other guys wouldn't go so hard on them the next time they started up in the locker room. It wasn't like I minded, but it was a little like letting my old babysitter, Savanna, the one in beauty school, try out her new eyeliners on me. Nice being touched, but nothing that "rings my chimes" (something else my *tío* says; he's really in love with my *tía*, thirty-five years, so he talks about that kind of thing a lot).

The boy in the sweatshirt passed in and out of the shadows. He had dark hair, almost black, so blue eyes, of course. Every *gringo* in the *gringo* town had light hair or light eyes or both. I went back to shaking rock salt and chili powder on my orange and didn't look up until he sat down near me in the grass.

He put his back against the tree trunk, pulled a blue water bottle out of his backpack, and drank it in one swallow. I was impressed. Couldn't help it. Mamá had bought me a red one at the Target—all these *gringas* carry them, she told me—and even though I hadn't filled it since that morning, it was still two-thirds full in my bag. Half of why Mamá got me hooked on cayenne and poblanos was to make sure I drank my water.

"What are you doing?" I asked.

He took a brown bag out of his backpack and set it on the grass. "Eating lunch."

"Here?"

"Is that a problem?"

His voice cracked a little, a quick pitch change and back like he'd gotten a cold for half a second. I couldn't help staring, couldn't help noticing that I couldn't find his Adam's apple, that his hands and feet were a little small, that he drank so much water so fast, like I'd heard guys like him ended up doing if they took testosterone.

He looked right at me, half smiled and nodded once. It was a respect kind of nod, like I'd just kicked his ass at chess or something. I'd clocked him, and he knew it. I wondered what his name had been as a girl.

"Say what you want about me," he said. "Word of advice, though. The gay jokes, not gonna fly around here."

"Yeah, I figured that out."

"We're so politically correct it kills us, so I'd keep it to yourself if you've got a problem. Trust me."

I couldn't help laughing at him. I always looked good and straight to anybody straight, but the other *tortilleras* and *playos* always made me. "You kidding?" I said.

He cocked his head a little, and I wondered if he was reading something in the way I wore my lipstick heavier and my hair messier than the other girls. Maybe he saw it in how I didn't wear blush or how my nail polish was chipped five days' worth, because straight girls never let it get like that.

Or maybe it was none of that, and he just saw in me what *los playos* always picked up, like a few stray threads off the same scarf. I meant to show him just those, but how he looked at me made me feel like he knew about the Danielas and Nikkis and Reynas. I'd left them behind, yes and no, because even the ones who wore baseball caps and boxers wouldn't go out anywhere our mothers might see, not with each other, and not with lipstick girls like me either.

"Got it," he said.

"Somebody's gonna say something about it. Might as well be me."

"Ever think that by saying something you're making it worse?" He threw the empty water bottle in his backpack and pulled out another one, blue plastic, same as the first one. He drank half of it before he even ate anything.

"Thirsty?" I asked.

He finished it, threw it in his backpack, took out another one. "Always."

He came back the next day, sat against the tree, drank his weight in water before he even touched his lunch. I watched him, not caring that the rudeness would've made Mamá pinch the back of my arm and tell me that good girls didn't stare.

He finished off the second one. "Ever see a doctor for that?"

"For what?" I asked.

"Chip on your shoulder," he said. "It'll give you back problems if you're not careful."

"So will carrying around four water bottles."

"I have to. I already fill them twice a day. If I didn't, I'd have eight with me."

Some wind tore through the tree, and the branches rained a few leaves. A couple of the wet ones caught in my hair and on my sweater. A laugh bubbled out of me like the fizzy off a bottle of Jarritos. Those leaves looked like peels off a gold orange.

"Am I gonna sound like a jerk if I say you're pretty when you smile?" he asked.

"No," I said. "But thanks anyway."

I couldn't get rid of him after that. People stared. Could've been bad stares, couldn't just been stares. Could've been about him, or me. Every chance I got, I stared back until they got too *nervioso* to keep looking.

After a week of lunches under that tree, he asked about the orange I brought every day.

"What are you putting on there?" he asked.

"It's chili powder." I cleared a bunch of the leaves from the grass so I could scoot a little closer. They were thick on the ground that day. "Wanna try it?"

"I'm not so good with spice," he said. "My cousin almost finished me off with a jalapeño."

"A jalapeño? That's as far as you got?"

He picked one of those little wet leaves out of my bangs, tucked a piece of my hair behind my ear.

Las tortilleras did what we had to do. Living. Adapting like moths turning brown to match trees. We made jokes so nobody else could, or if they did anyway, so we could say we did first. We kissed each other in the dark like our bodies couldn't take the light.

His hand strayed a little closer to mine in the grass until we touched different sides of the same leaf.

I ran my finger over the sliced orange. It shined with sugar and juice, shimmered with those little flecks of chili powder. I spread it over my mouth and kissed him, his breath catching at the heat and bite of those few bits of chili powder and rock salt shared between our mouths, sparse like stars over cities. It might've made him want more one day. I couldn't leave him thinking jalapeños were all there was. He had to know that *la especia* came in as many kinds as girls.

He kissed me back, taking the spice of my lips and tongue. They stared. Or I think they did. I don't know for sure. I didn't look back.

Graduation
Brighton Bennett

The night before graduation had a special feel to it. The fun of senior week was over. The raunchy, alcohol-filled nights at the bars and overactive daytime activities with friends had been replaced by the arrival of parents and the necessity to take showers and be presentable in public.

After the parents had been deposited at hotels in town, the fun began. The corner of campus that housed all the upperclassman dorms hummed with energy. Balcony doors had been thrown open in every unit while laughter and music floated from apartment to apartment.

Rachel and her roommates made their way through the building, chatting as they headed toward a second-floor apartment party. The girls who lived there were known for their ability to throw a rager, and welcomed Rachel's group with hugs and smiles.

"Come in! Can you *believe* how hot it is? There's beer in the kitchen. It's freezing cold, promise!"

The apartment was already full of people, and everyone was trying to suck the marrow out of the last night of college while escaping the oppressing heat of early June. Rachel went straight to the kitchen, getting a beer for herself and passing the cans out to her friends. As acquaintances wandered in and out, starting conversations and telling stories, she relaxed into the atmosphere. It felt good to get one last round of social calls in, to feel like she had left her mark on people. She shared her grad school plans with anyone who asked, and dutifully enquired about other people's post-graduation activities.

A half hour into the fun, her roommate Angela appeared. She tugged on Rachel's elbow and leaned in to whisper something in her ear.

"Emmerson's here. She's on the balcony."

Rachel was surprised. It was rare to run into Emmerson at an apartment party. She tossed the information around in her head, unsure of what to do with it. Rachel had made peace with Emmerson two years earlier—did she really want to risk diving in again? Yet even as she mulled it over, her feet walked her through the apartment toward the balcony. The humidity hit as soon as she slid the doors open, the cold of the apartment sealing off behind her.

Emmerson stood alone, gazing up at the stars. She was dressed like she always was: a pretty dress and pumps, a string of pearls around her neck. Rachel had seen her dressed like that a hundred times, lugging a giant tote bag around campus and looking perfectly presentable.

"Hey, Em."

Emmerson turned, a large smile on her face.

"Rachel. I thought you might show up."

Her voice was melodic, and a little deeper than usual, tinged with alcohol. Rachel was immediately swept back in time, remembering what else made Emmerson's voice husky.

"Are you here by yourself?"

"No, Heather's inside. Playing beer pong or something."

Rachel stepped farther onto the balcony to lean against

the railing, their elbows brushing minutely. She nodded at the information, mentally grouping people together. Heather, Emmerson's best friend, was in the same sorority as one of the girls who lived in the apartment.

"You look nice."

"Thanks. There was a…thing. With the trustees. Like a dinner thing."

As she stood there, smiling at Emmerson, Rachel was struck with all that had happened between them. All that had happened *for* each of them.

It was amazing, what a person could accomplish in four years—what one student could do on a small college campus. Rachel had watched from up close, and then afar, as Emmerson had transformed from a somewhat shy, uninvolved freshman to the most widely recognized name on campus.

Student body president. Vice president of the senior class. Resident advisor. Frequent appearances in the student newspaper through interviews or editorials. Honors student. Tutor.

The list went on and on and *on*.

There was no doubt about it; Emmerson was the darling of the college's administration, with a hand in every jar. She had a weekly appointment with the president, got coffee with the deans, made presentations to the board of trustees, and attended nearly every academic and student life social event that the college held.

People were often surprised when they found out about Rachel's connection to Emmerson Andrews. As a four-year cross-country runner, Rachel had avoided most of the student clubs and ran in a completely different social circle than Emmerson. Their interests and ambitions were miles apart, and they had practically nothing in common.

But Rachel did know Emmerson Andrews. She had known her better than anyone, at one point.

They had met on move-in day their freshman year, assigned to the same suite and living two doors down from each other. Rachel had instantly been attracted to Emmerson's easy laugh and infectious smile. Emmerson had seemed equally drawn to Rachel's quirky sense of humor and direct way of interacting. They had become best friends and constant companions, creating a happy little world in their suite that had spilled over to encompass a select few.

Then, after the Thanksgiving break, something changed. It hadn't felt as relaxed when they lay in bed together, talking about nonsense and avoiding homework. There had been a curious tension present when they hung out in the school's coffee shop, whiling away the hours between classes. An odd amount of eye contact had developed when they went to the library, staring at each other over Emmerson's political science textbooks and Rachel's anthropology readings.

Their friendship had evolved into something else entirely, filling each of them with an ache to constantly be closer. Maybe they had both known what was happening. Or maybe it had truly caught them by surprise. Rachel wasn't sure. She only remembered the feeling of absolute joy when Emmerson had leaned over one day and brushed their lips together.

It had tilted her world. They had held hands and stepped forward together, secure in the trust their friendship had created.

Tentatively, they had explored. Explored the feelings and emotions and what the pressure of Rachel's lips could do when Emmerson lay splayed on her back in her dorm bed, hands tightly clutching the sheets and neck arched up toward the ceiling, the glow in the dark plastic stars unavailable for viewing as her eyes scrunched shut in ecstasy. They had explored the way that Rachel's toes curled when Emmerson slid a finger inside, and the exquisite feeling of falling asleep in each other's arms, spent and exhausted, or demurely covered up and snuggled as Emmerson's roommate snored across the room.

Their world had been new and ripe for exploration.

There had been words spoken, perhaps too early, of love and forever and always. A life had been planned out, but the realistic mechanics needed to lay such plans had been blissfully ignored. They had believed that the world was theirs for the taking, with nothing else needed but to reach out and grab.

"Ray."

Rachel was startled out of her thoughts by Emmerson's soft smile, as if her once-lover knew exactly where her thoughts had been, as if Emmerson were reluctant to pull Rachel from the past.

"Sorry. Went to Mars for a minute."

They hadn't been alone together in over two years. Every so often there had been opportunities to catch up, when they would run into each other at the coffee shop, or when Rachel would end up behind Emerson in the line at the mailroom. On those occasions, they would ask generic questions, designed to be polite.

Rachel didn't often delve deep into memories of her time with Emmerson, but sometimes she allowed herself to remember the fun they'd had. In the winter they had bundled up to go sledding near the athletic fields with their dorm mates, returning completely soaked and red-faced from laughter and the cold. They had walked hand in hand to and from the library, always stopping under the magnolia tree on the quad for a quick embrace. In the spring, they had taken ice cream cones from the cafeteria to lay on the lawn outside their dorm, kissing away any stray droplets of sweetness. On hot nights in the freshman girls' dorm, they had lain around in undershirts and underwear, their hair wet from a shared shower. Toward the end of the term, they had taken to playing table tennis in the student lounge late at night, avoiding writing papers and doubling over in laughter at Emmerson's abysmal hand-eye coordination.

It had been a charmed semester—the happiest that either of them had ever had.

And, like most freshman romances, it didn't last.

Rachel had been too impatient, Emmerson too headstrong. Separated for the summer and divided by time zones, they had fallen into the heart-wrenching habit of fighting over the phone about stupid things, resentment building.

Upon their return to campus for sophomore year, Emmerson had begun to involve herself in more activities, constantly busy. Rachel had started to spend a lot more time with the girls on the cross-country team. She hadn't liked being "penciled in," and Emmerson hadn't liked being left out of the bond that the athletes had. As they grew apart, the fighting had increased.

By the time they returned from Thanksgiving break, it was over.

Devastatingly, unbelievably over.

It had been tough for Rachel to move on, believing at the time that she would never be able to love again—the dramatics of a twenty-year-old. Other girls had held no appeal.

That feeling had dissipated, and there had been other girls since Emmerson. Delightful, wonderful women who had drifted into and out of Rachel's life—and bed—teaching her about love and lust and everything that fell between.

As she stared at Emmerson in the soft light from the street lamp, Rachel realized that the first love was impossible to forget. Emmerson seemed to read her mind.

"Do you ever think about what would have happened if I hadn't been such a crazy bitch?"

Rachel laughed at the question. "Come on. You weren't that bad."

Emmerson's glance was knowing, and she shook her head a little, simultaneously swirling the liquid in her cup around. Vodka cranberry, if Rachel were to guess.

"I was terrible. A snotty little princess, I'm sure."

"You really weren't so bad."

Emmerson's gaze turned serious, the change making her look eighteen, not twenty-two, as if there was a distinct difference.

"I should have tried harder. Or something."

Her voice was soft, and pained, but the words were deliberate, as if she were used to tossing them around in her head often enough to become accustomed to them. Rachel felt the initial assault of emotion that accompanied reminiscing, but it subsided as quickly as it appeared. Hurt over Emmerson was long finished.

"There was nothing you could have done. Nothing that either of us could have done."

It had taken a year after their breakup for Rachel to understand that. The realization that sometimes people simply grow apart had been difficult for her to accept, but she had eventually understood. She had learned when to walk away with grace and an upbeat attitude.

"I miss you sometimes. Sorry, can I say that?"

A whimsical smile formed on Rachel's lips. Emmerson was always so proper, so correct. So formal, even.

"Yeah. You can say that."

"Good. Because I do. I...think about you sometimes."

Rachel moved her hand over, covering Emmerson's where it rested on the railing.

"I miss you too, sometimes."

She squeezed Emmerson's hand, enjoying the touch. The last physical contact between them had been their sophomore year, when they had been in the midst of breaking up. It felt good to touch Emmerson again. For a moment, she actually felt like a grown-up—acknowledging their past while nodding at the present.

"Are you excited about grad school? I can't even imagine starting up again in the fall."

Rachel removed her hand, running it through her light blond locks. They were shorter than usual. It was nice, in the heat.

"Yeah. I'm pretty excited. I mean, the fall feels far away. I'm not in training this summer, finally, so I can just relax. What about you? Anything interesting planned?"

Emmerson grinned, shrugging one shoulder. "I start at the firm in a week."

Rachel had read in the paper that Emmerson had scored a prestigious internship with a public relations firm in Washington D.C.—thanks to her relationships with the school's board of trustees, most likely.

"Sounds right up your alley."

"It is. It'll be good, I'm sure."

Emmerson's drive had to be admired. Rachel had been too focused on improving her cross-country time to fall in love with a high-powered career, but she had done well enough in her academics, and grad school would be a new adventure.

"You know, I never heard about you and anyone else."

On this last night of college, Rachel wanted to know, even if it wasn't her business.

"There weren't that many others. I mean there were a few, but mostly nothing serious."

Rachel stayed silent, waiting for Emmerson to continue.

"Um…there was the TA from my French class. But that ended up just being a few dates. And last year I hung out a lot with one of Heather's art friends, and in January I actually kind of dated one of the sophomores on the student government board. But nobody knows about that."

Her grin was infectious, and Rachel laughed, tipping her head to the side as she contemplated the scant dating history Emmerson revealed.

"That's, um…quite an assortment?"

Emmerson lifted one corner of her mouth, playing with the pearls around her neck.

"They were all women."

Rachel's mouth formed an *O*, her eyes widening. "I wasn't—"

"Of course you were. It's okay." Emmerson leaned closer. "How could I go back after us?"

The air was suddenly dry, all the moisture sucked by the electricity crackling between them. Emmerson reached a hand out, her fingertips landing on the back of Rachel's right hand. Ever so slightly, she traced a path from the middle of Rachel's wrist, over the middle knuckle, to the tip of her finger. Her touch was light, enticing, and it made Rachel's entire body open up on the inside.

Rachel tipped her head back just a little, then turned her attention to the right. Emmerson met her gaze unsmiling, her eyes issuing an invitation that she hadn't offered in a long time.

It came flooding back in a moment. The way Emmerson's hands felt on her body. The ways they'd made each other dizzy with pleasure. The way it felt to fall apart in Emmerson's arms, anchored only by the emerald green of her eyes. It hadn't been polite, between them—it had been messy and hot and sweaty, both of them taking greedily and giving generously.

It was a lot to remember, and Rachel could feel her body responding accordingly. Closing her eyes and taking a deep breath, she concentrated on her swirling emotions. Was she interested in going down that road? Again? She had wanted to talk to Emmerson and say good-bye; presented with more, she wasn't sure what to do.

Rachel removed her hand from Emmerson's touch, taking a half step backward as she looked toward the apartment.

"I should probably find the girls. They wanted to hit up another party tonight."

If Emmerson was disappointed, she didn't show it. The polite, public face was back and Rachel exhaled slowly in regret. Needing to ease the moment away from the precipice it teetered on, she tried for comedy.

"Are you gonna take your turn with Heather?" The teasing note in Rachel's voice made Emmerson blush.

"I'm about as good at beer pong as I am at ping-pong. I'm actually going to head home. I had a breakfast at seven this morning and I'm exhausted. And unpacked."

Rachel rolled her eyes. "You can't turn in early on the last night of college. Besides, lineup isn't until ten tomorrow."

"I know. But pictures start at nine, and I have to be there for that. Plus I need to do some packing or my dad will have a fit. I'm glad I got to see you tonight."

Emmerson put her hand on Rachel's shoulder. Her touch

felt warm, doubly so because of the temperature. It burned Rachel's bare skin.

She closed her eyes as Emmerson leaned in and hugged her, inhaling the scent of her perfume. It felt good to be in her arms again, two years of distance melting away easily. Rachel's hands held Emmerson's upper back tightly, both of them taking the moment for their big good-bye.

"You're the best, Ray. You always were."

Her whispered words caused Rachel to shiver, and they pulled apart.

"You too, Em."

Together, they walked back into the apartment, where the air had been turned up to accommodate the crowd of people. Rachel's roommates were standing near the coffee table, drinking and laughing, and she walked to them, ignoring the curious glances they sent her way. Her mind was spinning, awash with the possibilities she had turned down. Emmerson had been offering one last night—a capstone, of sorts, on their time together.

It had been the right thing, to walk away. Rachel wasn't looking for a quick fuck or the heartbreak of starting up something again; of bringing all the emotions back to the surface.

And yet...

Things had always felt a bit unsettled between them. They had been the best of friends before their relationship, and it had felt wrong to separate with no lingering affection. Perhaps one last night together would be the cherry on top—the balm on any residual hurt. For a few minutes the thoughts bounced around her head, weakening her resolve. She couldn't help but think about being with Emmerson again, older, wiser, and more experienced. Would their chemistry have dissipated in the two years since their breakup? Or would they be more combustible than ever?

"Listen…I'm gonna catch you guys later."

She had no interest in waiting to see what her friends would say. Instead, she dipped out of the group and glanced around the apartment to see if Emmerson had already left. When there was no sign of her, Rachel maneuvered her way through the apartment and made her way out of the building. The gravel crunched under her feet as she picked up her pace.

As she stepped onto the sidewalk, she caught sight of Emmerson about to cross the street. As if instinctively, Emmerson turned, and Rachel jogged down the sidewalk, hands stuck in the front pockets of her jeans. Neither of them said anything until she stopped, leaving just a few feet between them.

"I'll walk with you."

For a long moment they stood there as Emmerson considered the offer. She reached out a hand and put it on Rachel's cheek, her thumb stroking the curve of the bone. Rachel accepted the caress but made no movement, her gaze trained on Emmerson's green eyes.

The air around them seemed heavy with promise. Rachel could feel her heart pounding.

"Okay."

On the other side of the street the crosswalk gave way into a long and winding brick path, which led by the library toward the other side of the residential campus. They walked slowly, silent for a long while, Emmerson's heels clicking on the brick.

"Can you believe this is really it? Freshman year seems like a million years ago."

Unlocking the door, Emmerson ignored the overhead fluorescent light, finding her way in the dark to the five-headed lamp that was set up next to her bed. It put a soft glow over the room, throwing shades of red and yellow and pink onto the walls. The room was as put-together and lived-in as it would be during the middle of the semester.

"Uh, wow. You weren't kidding. Why are you so bad at packing?"

"I mean, I have clothes and stuff packed. I was just so busy this week."

"Only *you* could be busy during senior week."

"I was wrapping up loose ends. And the trustee meetings. Graduation details. All that crap. I have Diet Coke."

"Sure."

As Emmerson retrieved the soft drinks from her fridge, Rachel looked around. There were picture frames all over, displaying smiling photographs of Emmerson with her friends from high school, and on the corkboard was a picture of their entire crew from freshman year. Rachel could see her eighteen-year-old self, staring back at her with wide eyes and a smug grin. She shook her head and turned her back on the photo, accepting the drink.

"Thanks."

Toeing off her pumps, Emmerson sat on the edge of her bed, the bright floral pattern of her dress contrasting with the gray watercolor flowers printed on her comforter. The skin above the bust of her dress had flushed in the heat, the hairs at the crown of her head curling a little.

"Come sit."

Rachel sat at the foot of the bed as Emmerson slid back to the headboard, leaning against her assortment of pillows. They stared at each other, both predators for a moment, wondering who would be the prey. The pressure from the kiss downstairs had dissipated, leaving them on different sides of an emotional void. Suddenly surround by Emmerson's world, Rachel felt a little unsure.

"Why'd you invite me up?"

"Why'd you walk me home?"

The smile pulled at Rachel's lips slowly, but she narrowed her eyes. It was different to play the game with Em, after so long. Before, their passion had been sparked by a touch or a look, always welcomed. The verbal game they had been playing since she encountered Emmerson on the balcony was new territory for them.

"Can I ask something?"

"Sure."

Emmerson waited till Rachel looked up before asking. "Do you regret breaking up?"

Rachel glanced at the corkboard. The 4x6 photograph was small from her vantage point on the bed, but she could still make out her smiling, happy face. She turned back to Emmerson, mentally pulling herself out of the past.

"No. I don't."

To her surprise, Emmerson smiled. "Good. Neither do I...I regret not being able to love you more, or longer...But I think it was what we both needed."

"I'm sorry I couldn't recognize that at the time."

She had caused Emmerson a lot of pain in her refusal to accept that they weren't "meant to be." Hurtful things had been said, and what could have been a very clean and amicable break had been jagged and drawn out over the course of a semester.

"It wasn't your fault. Half-share, okay?"

Half-share. Emmerson used to say that as she peeled an

orange, or opened a candy bar, offering it out. Rachel hadn't heard or thought about the expression in two years. There were a million things about Emmerson that she had forgotten.

Emmerson extended her hand, the movement smooth, assured.

"C'mere."

Rachel took the offered hand, crawling up the bed on all fours. Emmerson shifted, lying on her side, and Rachel mimicked her pose, also placing her head on the pillow. Their noses almost touched, and from so close, she could see the lamplight reflected in Emmerson's deep green eyes. She reached over and put the can on the bedside table.

"Will this hurt in the morning?"

Emmerson's voice was inquisitive, like a child asking a nurse if a shot will hurt. Four years earlier, Rachel would have said no; *no, it won't hurt*, assuring and cajoling Emmerson all at once.

"I don't know. It might."

Rachel reached out to trace the lips that she had kissed so many times. It was familiar to be so close, but not the same as it used to be. She was a different person than she'd been when they met. They were both different people. Would she fall in love with the Emmerson of senior year? Busy, political, savvy...

"I'm okay with that...if it hurts. Later."

Rachel considered her options. She had tried to run Emmerson out of her system two years earlier. It hadn't worked, but eventually she had been able to move on. Falling back into Emmerson's embrace might hurt her heart in the morning, but Rachel had made her decision the moment she'd left the party to run after Emmerson. There was no turning back.

She missed the heat. There had been a warmth to being

with Emmerson that she hadn't found with anyone else; a fire that had blazed in and around them, and kept her constantly warm, constantly on an edge. She wanted to feel the heat again. No matter the consequences.

"I am, too."

The smile that Emmerson gave her was encouraging and lovely, and Rachel let herself fall into the embrace without reservations. With aching slowness, they began to kiss, reacquainting themselves. Mere brushing of lips gave way to tender pressure, and it then transformed into something more aggressive and possessive. Rachel melted under Emmerson's insistent caresses, opening her mouth, searching with her hands. Emmerson's skin burned under her touch, as if her fingers were leaving lines of fire in their wake. Her skin was salty under Rachel's lips.

Before she was too far gone, Emmerson reached over to turn off the lamp, plunging the room into semidarkness. The light from the street lamp outside her window bled across the bed, leaving them illuminated enough to see.

A gust of breeze blew through the window screen, but stopped just as suddenly, making the room feel even more stifling. Rachel felt scorched by the heat, inside and out and all over her mind. It had always been like that with Emmerson.

Emmerson sighed. "It's so hot."

Rachel smiled against her neck.

It always was.

CONTRIBUTORS

BRENNA HARVEY is a writer and queer intersectional feminist activist from New England. She is currently pursuing graduate studies in sociology at the University of Connecticut, where her main areas of interest are human rights theory, gender identity, and sexual and reproductive health. Though an aspiring social scientist, she actually believes that only fiction has the power to speak meaningful truth.

JUSTINE F. LANE is a vegetarian, Japan-obsessed type who lives with a black cat she picked up in a seedy area and her partner, whom she picked up somewhere else. Her ultimate goal in life is to have a private island and/or biodynamic farm with a queer organic café. While waiting for that to materialize, she writes stuff, edits stuff, and teaches stuff. In her spare time, she collects herbal teas, studies spices, and gorges herself on Indian sweets. This is her first short story to be published. You can mail her at: meanderinglane@gmail.com.

TOMMY GRAZIANO was born and raised in Sacramento, California, and started writing in fourth grade. Since then, he has attended the California State Summer School for the Arts program, served as editor-in-chief of his high school newspaper, and has conducted an internship at the *Roseville Press-Tribune*. He has plans to study creative writing at San Francisco State University.

A.J. SLATER is living at home as she attends college; home to her is a little town in southern Indiana. She is studying criminology with a minor in English writing. A.J.'s three main hobbies are sports, reading, and writing. She has two dogs, two sisters (middle child), and two very supportive parents. A.J. is planning to go into law enforcement with a special interest in the K-9 unit. She has an imagination with no boundaries and hopes to be able to use it more in her writing. "Crystal Crisis" is her first publication.

OLIVIA DZIWAK is a Canadian writer who identifies as a stress-ridden young adult, hesitant poet, and post–theatre school student. She hails from suburban Ontario, where she lives with a fantastically supportive family that is as opinionated and rant-inclined as she is. Olivia begins study at the University of Toronto in the fall of 2012 and will empower herself with fearsome political science knowledge in hopes of being well prepared for furthering LGBTQ equality and [democratically!] conquering the world in general. She also intends to remain a writer and is buoyed that her short stories have been published in various youth magazines, zines, and the *Toronto Star*.

ASHLEY BARTLETT was born and raised in California. She is from Sacramento and her life consists of reading and writing. Most of the time Ashley engages in these pursuits while sitting in front of a coffee shop with her girlfriend and smoking cigarettes. It's a glamorous life. She is an obnoxious, sarcastic punk-ass, but her friends don't hold that against her.

She currently lives in Long Beach, but you can find her at ashbartlett.com.

JULIE R. SANCHEZ is a California native and a student at the University of Pennsylvania, where she studies cultural anthropology and gender studies. Although she writes mostly long-form fiction, her short fiction has been published in *First Call* and the *FWord*. She has received the Tim Hurley Writing Award and currently works on the fiction staff of the *Adroit Journal*.

If you asked people who **WARREN SMITH** was, they would all give you the same answer. He is just a skinny young boy living in a small town waiting for his chance to play in the city.

KIRSTY LOGAN is a fiction writer, journalist, literary magazine editor, teacher, book reviewer, arts intern, and general layabout. She recently completed her first novel, *Rust and Stardust*, and a short story collection, *The Rental Heart and Other Fairytales*. Her work has been published in over 80 anthologies and literary magazines, including *Best British Short Stories 2011* (Salt), and broadcast on BBC Radio 4. She has a semicolon tattooed on her toe and lives in Glasgow with her girlfriend. Say hello at kirstylogan.com.

SAM SOMMER is the author of *Reservations for 4*, a one-act play that was presented this March as part of the 2012 Downtown Urban Theatre Festival, and *Bed & Breakfast*, a new gay comedy presented as part of the 2008 NY Fresh Fruit Festival and winner of Best Full-Length Play. His short stories have been published in numerous anthologies. Most recently, "Color Zap!" in *Queer Fish*, "Human Nature" in

Gay and Gray, "Starting Over" in *Best Gay Romance 2009*, and "Nightdance," the lead story in *Quickies III*, short fiction on gay male desire.

JOSEPH AVIV is a graduate student interested in intersections between queer displacement and the dynamics of families and cultural heritages. He has lived in New York, Massachusetts, and Israel. He holds a BA in art from a small liberal arts college, where he also studied psychology and literature. His MA is in gender studies and Jewish studies, and he is currently pursuing a PhD in Jewish literature.

AIMEE LUKES is a twenty-year-old college student in Chicago. In high school, she started a GSA. She enjoys writing, cats, long walks on the beach, and screaming matches on the Internet.

ANDREW ARSLAN is a full-time college student studying English literature & the law at John Jay College of Criminal Justice in New York City. He is a real estate agent with Next Step Realty and a writer for Intellectualyst.com. You can also follow him on Twitter: @AndrewArslan.

Born in Melbourne, Florida, **ARIANA MONTOYA** has lived there for the entirety of her twenty years. From an early age, she was dictating stories to her older sister, and she began writing poetry by six. Now she is attending college with the ultimate goal of becoming a middle school history teacher, and working retail. However, she has never forgotten her love of the written word and continues to write.

ARCHER DARKE is a twenty-one-year-old oddball from Manchester, England, who likes to spend her free time indoors where the famously bad English weather can't reach her. Her hobbies include eating, sleeping, and ensuring her hamster doesn't find a new way to escape (again), and when she's not concentrating on those she's busy repairing and painting cars in order to pay the bills. This is her first short story to be published. You can e-mail her at ArcherDarke@hotmail.co.uk.

REBEKAH WEATHERSPOON is the author of *Better Off Red*, the first installment in the Vampire Sorority Sister Series published by Bold Strokes Books. She lives in Southern California but longs for the shores of New Hampshire and Maine.

ANNA MEADOWS writes from her heritage in the Mexican-American Southwest and her passion for stories about women in love. Her work has appeared in numerous anthologies. She lives with her Sapphic husband in California.

BRIGHTON BENNETT lives in Chicago and never wants to leave the Midwest. She loves Thai food, Cardinals baseball, her girlfriend, and all things lovely. She collects miniature elephants, bakes a delicious loaf of banana chocolate chip bread, and is constantly trying to keep all the plants in her apartment alive. This is her first published work, and she's thrilled about it. She is always on the lookout for a new pen pal, so send her a line at brighton.bennett@gmail.com.

About the Editors

Radclyffe has written over forty romance and romantic intrigue novels, dozens of short stories, and, writing as L.L. Raand, has authored a paranormal romance series, The Midnight Hunters.

She is an eight-time Lambda Literary Award finalist in romance, mystery and erotica—winning in both romance (*Distant Shores, Silent Thunder*) and erotica (*Erotic Interludes 2: Stolen Moments* edited with Stacia Seaman and *In Deep Waters 2: Cruising the Strip* written with Karin Kallmaker). A member of the Saints and Sinners Literary Hall of Fame, she is also a 2010 RWA/FF&P Prism award winner for *Secrets in the Stone*. Her 2011 title *Firestorm* is a ForeWord Review Book of the Year award finalist. She is also the president of Bold Strokes Books, one of the world's largest independent LGBT publishing companies.

Dr. Katherine E. Lynch teaches English literature and composition at a small college in the SUNY system. She writes romance novels for Bold Strokes Books under the name Nell Stark. Her novels include *Running With the Wind* (2007) and *Homecoming* (2008), and the everafter series (co-written with Trinity Tam).

Soliloquy Titles From Bold Strokes Books

Sara by Greg Herren. A mysterious and beautiful new student at Southern Heights High School stirs things up when students start dying. (978-1-60282-674-8)

Boys of Summer, edited by Steve Berman. Stories of young love and adventure, when the sky's ceiling is a bright blue marvel, when another boy's laughter at the beach can distract from dull summer jobs. (978-1-60282-663-2)

Street Dreams by Tama Wise. Tyson Rua has more than his fair share of problems growing up in New Zealand—he's gay, he's falling in love, and he's run afoul of the local hip-hop crew leader just as he's trying to make it as a graffiti artist. (978-1-60282-650-2)

me@you.com by K.E. Payne. Is it possible to fall in love with someone you've never met? Imogen Summers thinks so because it's happened to her. (978-1-60282-592-5)

Swimming to Chicago by David-Matthew Barnes. As the lives of the adults around them unravel, high school students Alex and Robby form an unbreakable bond, vowing to do anything to stay together—even if it means leaving everything behind. (978-1-60282-572-7)

Speaking Out edited by Steve Berman. Inspiring stories written for and about LGBT and Q teens of overcoming adversity (against intolerance and homophobia) and experiencing life after "coming out." (978-1-60282-566-6)

365 Days by K.E. Payne. Life sucks when you're seventeen years old and confused about your sexuality, and the girl of your dreams doesn't even know you exist. Then in walks sexy new emo girl, Hannah Harrison. Clemmie Atkins has exactly 365 days to discover herself, and she's going to have a blast doing it! (978-1-60282-540-6)

Cursebusters! by Julie Smith. Budding psychic Reeno is the most accomplished teenage burglar in California, but one tiny screw-up and poof!—she's sentenced to Bad Girl School. And that isn't even her worst problem. Her sister Haley's dying of an illness no one can diagnose, and now she can't even help. (978-1-60282-559-8)

Who I Am by M.L. Rice. Devin Kelly's senior year is a disaster. She's in a new school in a new town, and the school bully is making her life miserable—but then she meets his sister Melanie and realizes her feelings for her are more than platonic. (978-1-60282-231-3)

Sleeping Angel by Greg Herren. Eric Matthews survives a terrible car accident only to find out everyone in town thinks he's a murderer—and he has to clear his name even though he has no memories of what happened. (978-1-60282-214-6)

Mesmerized by David-Matthew Barnes. Through her close friendship with Brodie and Lance, Serena Albright learns about the many forms of love and finds comfort for the grief and guilt she feels over the brutal death of her older brother, the victim of a hate crime. (978-1-60282-191-0)

The Perfect Family by Kathryn Shay. A mother and her gay son stand hand in hand as the storms of change engulf their perfect family and the life they knew. (978-1-60282-181-1)

Father Knows Best by Lynda Sandoval. High school juniors and best friends Lila Moreno, Meryl Morganstern, and Caressa Thibodoux plan to make the most of the summer before senior year. What they discover that amazing summer about girl power, growing up, and trusting friends and family more than prepares them to tackle that all-important senior year! (978-1-60282-147-7)